THE CURSE OF THE ANCIENT EMERALD

#9 *THE CURSE OF THE ANCIENT EMERALD*

FRANKLIN W. DIXON

ALADDIN New York London Toronto Sydney New Delhi

ALADDIN

An imprint of Simon & Schuster Children's Publishing Division

1230 Avenue of the Americas, New York, NY 10020

This Aladdin hardcover edition June 2015

Text copyright © 2015 by Simon & Schuster, Inc.

Jacket illustration copyright © 2015 by Kevin Keele

Also available in an Aladdin paperback edition.

All rights reserved, including the right of reproduction in whole or in part in any form.

ALADDIN is a trademark of Simon & Schuster, Inc.,

and related logo is a registered trademark of Simon & Schuster, Inc.

THE HARDY BOYS MYSTERY STORIES, HARDY BOYS ADVENTURES,

and related logo are trademarks of Simon & Schuster, Inc.

For information about special discounts for bulk purchases, please contact

Simon & Schuster Special Sales at 1-866-506-1949 or business@simonandschuster.com.

The Simon & Schuster Speakers Bureau can bring authors to your live event.

For more information or to book an event contact the Simon & Schuster Speakers Bureau

at 1-866-248-3049 or visit our website at www.simonspeakers.com.

Jacket designed by Karin Paprocki

The text of this book was set in Adobe Caslon Pro.

Manufactured in the United States of America 0515 FFG

2 4 6 8 10 9 7 5 3 1

Library of Congress Control Number 2014945583

ISBN 978-1-4814-2476-9 (hc)

ISBN 978-1-4814-2475-2 (pbk)

ISBN 978-1-4814-2477-6 (eBook)

CONTENTS

THE EMERALD OF ASTARA

1

FRANK

AND HERE," SAID THE MUSEUM GUIDE with the little smile that meant he was about to treat us to *another* terrible joke, "we have the—ha-ha—*jewel* in the crown of our collection, the Emerald of Astara."

I fought down a groan as he waited expectantly for the class to acknowledge his amazing sense of humor. This guy was *terrible*.

"Don't give up the day job," called someone from the back of the group.

Our school chaperone, Mr. Sweeney, swiveled around and fixed Neal "Neanderthal" Bunyan with his laser glare.

"Busted," muttered my brother, Joe.

1

Neanderthal's grin faded under Mr. Sweeney's withering look.

"Sorry, sir," he mumbled.

"The Emerald of Astara," said the tour guide, determined not to be derailed from his lecture, "is over two thousand five hundred years old and can be traced back to ancient Persia—that's modern-day Iran to you."

I whistled appreciatively and leaned in to inspect the egg-size jewel. Hidden lights inside the glass case made the green stone twinkle and glint. It looked like something Indiana Jones would fight to get his hands on.

"The jewel is believed to be cursed—"

"Really?" interrupted Joe. "What kind of curse?"

Joe had been looking pretty bored since the class arrived at the Bayport History Museum for our school trip. But talk of an ancient curse was enough to get him interested.

"It was given to the sultan of Astara as a gift," said the guide. "He was said to be obsessed with it, never letting the jewel out of his sight. He was found dead only a week later, clutching the jewel to his chest."

"How did he die?" I asked.

"The curse," said Joe. "*Duh.* Aren't you listening?"

"People don't die from curses." I snorted.

"What about Tutankhamen?" remarked Chet Morton, our best friend. "All those people who died after opening King Tut's tomb?"

"King Tut's Tomb," repeated Joe, grinning at Amber Arlington. "Cool name for a band."

Amber smiled back at Joe, and I fought down a little twinge of jealousy. Amber was new in our class and had taken to hanging out with us in the cafeteria and at our favorite coffee shop, the Meet Locker. She was smart, funny, and *incredibly* good-looking—the complete package. I'm not usually the type to run off chasing girls— that's Joe's thing—but there was something different about Amber.

"Actually," I said, "the curse of Tutankhamen is an urban legend. Out of the twenty-six people who were there when the tomb was opened, only six died."

"Six is a lot!" protested Chet.

"Yeah, but they died over the course of a decade. The talk of a curse started when the financier of the dig was bitten by a mosquito. The bite became infected, and he died of blood poisoning."

"Didn't Sir Arthur Conan Doyle believe in the curse?" asked Amber.

I *knew* I was right about her. Looks *and* brains. "He sure did. Kinda weird, huh? The creator of Sherlock Holmes— the most analytical detective in history—believing in curses and magic. He was a well-known believer in the occult."

"It's *so* cool that you know all that," said Amber.

I felt heat in my cheeks. "It's nothing. I just like to read up on history."

Joe grabbed me by the neck and tried to give me a noogie. "Yeah, my brother the egghead."

"Joe Hardy!" snapped Mr. Sweeney. "Have you and your brother finished acting like five-year-olds?"

I heard the rest of the class snickering. Amber shook her head in a mock sorrowful motion and wagged her finger at us.

"I apologize for my students," Mr. Sweeney told the guide. "It seems their parents didn't teach them about such things as manners. Please continue."

"Um, thank you," said the guide. "The emerald was lent to us by the New York Metropolitan Museum of Art, but we had to install a state-of-the-art security system before they would even *consider* letting us have it. I can't go into too many details, but it really is quite a phenomenal piece of technology."

"I bet Catwoman could steal it," said Joe.

The tour guide smiled. "I think even Selina Kyle would have trouble getting her hands on this prize," he said.

I raised my eyebrows. I was surprised he even knew who Catwoman *was*.

The guide pointed to the ceiling. "Motion sensors that are sensitive enough to pick up the presence of a mouse. Heat sensors that detect not only a change in temperature, but human pheromones in sweat as well." He smiled at Joe's look of surprise, then pointed to the floor. "Motion sensors in a ten-foot square around the case." He pointed at the wall. "Infrared grid. And no," he said, arching his eyebrows

4

as Joe opened his mouth, "a robber *cannot* maneuver his or her way around the sensor beams, no matter how acrobatic he or she is. This is a three-dimensional lattice cube. Each beam creates a gap no smaller than a dime, and it completely surrounds the case."

Joe whistled. "I'm impressed."

"Then my day has not been a total waste," said the guide with a bright, slightly sarcastic smile. "Now, if you all care to follow me, we can take a peek behind the scenes at where we restore some of our damaged works of art."

I fell into step beside Joe.

"She's really something, isn't she?" asked Joe, nodding his head toward Amber, who was a few paces ahead of us.

"Who?" I asked innocently.

Chet squeezed between us and threw his arms over our shoulders. "How long do you think this will take?" he complained. "I'm starving."

"You're *always* starving," said Joe.

"It's not my fault!" protested Chet. "I have a very fast metabolism."

The tour guide stopped before a door with a sign saying STAFF ONLY. KEEP OUT. He unlocked the door and led us into a narrow corridor. I peered into rooms as we passed them, curious about what was kept back here, but it wasn't very interesting—offices and storerooms, mostly.

The guide finally stopped before a heavy wooden door.

"I must ask you not to touch anything in this room," he

said. "The pieces are here for repair, and any disturbances could be catastrophic for the museum."

Mr. Sweeney glared at us to reinforce the words, and the guide opened the door.

The room beyond was huge, illuminated by long strips of lights that hung from steel ceiling beams. There were no windows anywhere, which I assumed was a security thing. Off to our left was a long workbench where somebody was painstakingly cleaning an old pottery vase using something that smelled of strong chemicals.

"Welcome to the exciting world of art restoration," announced the guide proudly.

"Riveting, don't you agree?" whispered Amber to my left.

"Oh, yes," I said, my face deadpan. "Very."

Amber snorted with laughter, then blushed bright red and slapped a hand over her mouth.

I grinned at her, then realized we had been left behind. The rest of the tour had moved deeper into the room, stopping before a painting mounted on an easel. A man who looked to be in his fifties was leaning close to the piece, a tiny brush in his hand.

The painting depicted a ruined boat sinking off a rocky coast. The sky was filled with storm clouds, but just to the right the sun was breaking through, pillars of bright light striking the waves. The upper-right portion of the painting, where the sun was visible, was vibrant—obviously where the painting had been restored. But the rest of the picture was dull and muted.

"This is *Sun Greets Shipwreck* by the brothers Johannes and Friedrich von Esling," said the guide. "It's worth over one hundred thousand dollars. Mr. Ramone here has been working on it for two months now."

"Maybe someone else should take over," muttered Neanderthal. "They'd be quicker."

Mr. Ramone turned to stare at us. He was wearing these weird glasses with majorly thick lenses in them, giving him the look of a surprised owl.

"Oh, no," said the guide. "Mr. Ramone is actually one of the faster restorers. He should be finished with this painting by the end of the year."

"Nice job if you can get it," said Neanderthal.

The tour guide glared at Neanderthal, who was snickering with the other jocks. "It takes *years* for an artist to become qualified as a restorer. It is a complex job that requires natural talent, patience, and a mature mind."

"That's three strikes for Neal, then," Joe murmured into my ear.

I was about to reply when the room was suddenly plunged into darkness.

"Don't panic," barked the tour guide. "Just a power surge. The generator will start up—"

He was cut off by a startled cry of pain. I heard a clattering sound, a grunt, and a scuffle, then something breaking.

"What's happening?" demanded Mr. Sweeney. "Neal, if this is your doing, I'll put you in detention for a month!"

"It's not me, sir!" Neal shouted.

"Everyone stand still," I called out, fishing around in my pocket for my phone. It looked like the rest of the group had the same idea, because a second later the room was filled with the white glow of our screens.

I pointed mine in the direction the noise had come from.

Mr. Ramone, the restorer, was lying unconscious on the floor, a trickle of blood clearly visible on his bald head.

"Someone call an ambulance!" yelled Joe. "Oh. Hang on, I have my own phone."

He shifted his phone so that he could dial 911. As he did, I noticed something else: The painting that had been resting on the easel was gone!

I whirled around, searching the room. Amber must have seen the same thing, because she took a step away from the rest of the class, peering into the darkness.

"There!" she said.

I looked to where she was pointing and saw a black-clad figure running toward the door. He had a ski mask pulled over his face and wore what looked like night-vision goggles—the kind that army rangers use on evening patrols. He held the painting beneath his arm as he dodged around the workbench and vanished through the door.

"Stop, thief!" I shouted, and sprinted after him.

THE CHASE 2

"STOP, THIEF!"

I looked on in amazement as Frank tore after a masked figure. Where had *he* come from?

I saw the empty easel, realized what was happening, then ran after them. I overtook Frank before we even reached the door; I always have been a better athlete.

The thief ducked into a storeroom. I picked up speed and arrived a few steps behind him.

As I entered the room, I caught a brief glimpse of something flying through the air toward me. I ducked instinctively, narrowly avoiding a heavy box that smashed against the door frame, showering me with wood splinters and shards of pottery. I hoped that whatever was in there wasn't too valuable.

I kept low and rolled forward, bumping to a halt behind a huge storage crate. Frank appeared in the doorway, and I gestured frantically for him to get down. He dropped to all fours and crawled into the room.

I peered around the side of the crate. There was another door at the far end of the room, and it was swinging shut.

"Come on!"

I scrambled to my feet, Frank close behind. The door led into another, narrower passage, the walls covered in heating pipes. There was a set of stairs at the end, and the thief was already halfway up them.

Frank and I sprinted after him, taking the stairs two at a time. We burst out into bright daylight. I paused, shielding my eyes with my hand.

We were on the roof of the museum. I could see downtown Bayport sprawling around us on all sides. The thief was standing at the edge of the roof, stuffing the painting into some sort of bag. Which he then threw into the air.

But it didn't drop. At least, not right away. A parachute opened, and the painting floated slowly down and out of sight. Then the thief turned to Frank and me, saluted, and fell backward into the air.

"No!" shouted Frank, running forward in a vain attempt to catch him. But he was way too late; the guy would be a pancake by now.

There was a slithering sound to my left. I looked around and saw a pile of orange rope rapidly unraveling. One end was tied to a rock-climbing bolt that had been embedded into the roof, and the other end was sliding over the edge of the building. It stopped suddenly with a barely heard *twang*. I knew that sound. I'd heard the same thing when Frank and I had gone bungee jumping from the Bayport Bridge. I hurried to the edge of the roof and stared down.

The thief was hanging by the bungee cord a few feet above the ground. He pulled himself up, grabbed the cord with one hand, then used a knife to cut it from around his ankle with the other. He dangled from the rope for a second, then dropped lightly to the ground.

He got to his feet, grabbed the painting, and ran away down the alley, tearing off his mask in the process. But he was too far away for me to get a good look at him.

I slapped the lip of the roof, then turned to stare at Frank in frustration.

"You're home a little early. How was the field trip?" asked Aunt Trudy as Frank and I trudged through the kitchen door about three hours later.

I went to the fridge while Frank flopped down at the table.

"Well, there was some trouble at the museum," I said.

"Oh, dear. Nothing serious, I hope."

"Actually, it was," said Frank. "A robbery. The whole class had to give witness statements."

"You should have seen it, Aunt Trudy," I said, taking

a can of soda from the fridge. "This guy had these really sick night-vision goggles. He was dressed in black. Frank and I chased him onto the roof. It was like a James Bond movie."

"You chased him?" said Aunt Trudy, eyebrows raised. "Isn't that a little dangerous?"

"You know us, Aunt Trudy." I chuckled. "Danger's our middle name!"

"Well, it's not meant to be. Now, did you have lunch? I have some lasagna in the fridge. I kept some food for you both."

There's no arguing with Aunt Trudy when she wants to feed you. Not that I'd *want* to argue. Her food is amazing. I sat down opposite Frank.

"So what happened after you chased him?" asked Aunt Trudy.

"He had this amazing parachute bag that he stashed the stolen painting in," I said. "Just threw it off the roof. Then he jumped after it."

"And did *he* have a parachute?"

"No," answered Frank. "The roof wasn't high enough for a full-size parachute to deploy. You need to be at least two hundred feet up to do that."

"That's good to know," said Aunt Trudy. "In case I ever get the urge to take up parachuting."

"This guy had a bungee cord," I said. "He jumped right into space."

"You don't have to sound like you admire him so much," muttered Frank.

"Oh, come on!" I protested. "It *was* kinda cool."

Aunt Trudy placed two heaping plates in front of us. I paused to take in the heavenly aroma of her homemade lasagna before digging in.

"Did you catch him?" asked Aunt Trudy.

"Afraid not," said Frank, toying with his food. "He had too much of a head start."

"Plus, you know, the whole leaping-off-the-roof thing," I said around a mouthful of food. "Hard to keep up with that."

The front doorbell rang. I stood up, but Aunt Trudy waved me back to my seat.

"Eat. I'll get it."

I wolfed down the rest of my food and nodded at Frank's plate. "You going to eat that?"

He slid the plate across to me. "Knock yourself out. Not really hungry."

Aunt Trudy returned with an envelope. "For both of you."

"Mail at this time?" said Frank in surprise, examining the envelope.

"It was a courier service. I had to sign on one of those horrible screen things."

Frank held up the envelope and raised his eyebrows questioningly.

"Go ahead," I said. I was still eating, and nothing gets in the way when I'm eating.

Frank opened the envelope and pulled out a single sheet of paper. I paused, a forkful of meat and pasta halfway to my mouth. I could see by the look on his face that it was bad news.

"What's wrong?" I asked.

Frank wordlessly slid the paper across the table. It was a short note made from letters cut out of newspapers and magazines.

Shame you didn't crack the riddle.
You could have stopped this.

Underneath these two sentences was a URL.

I glanced at Frank. He nodded, and we rose from the table.

"What about dessert?" cried Aunt Trudy as we hurried from the kitchen. "It's apple pie!"

"Keep it warm, Aunt T," I called back. "We'll be back in a minute."

We went into Frank's room, and he sat down in front of his computer. He typed the URL into his browser. When the page loaded, I couldn't believe my eyes. It was a video of the stolen painting!

Frank pushed play, and we watched in horror as something was sprayed across the painting from off camera. Then we heard a scratching noise, and a match suddenly appeared, flying through the air.

The painting erupted in flames.

"No way," I said breathlessly.

The canvas started to bubble and peel, the boat and waves turning black. The fire raged for about thirty seconds, and by the end of the clip there was absolutely nothing left of *Sun Greets Shipwreck*.

"How much did the tour guide say that painting was worth?" Frank whispered.

"A hundred thousand dollars."

Frank studied the note while I replayed the clip, wondering if it was a fake. But I didn't think it was. This painting had the exact same section in the upper right-hand corner that Mr. Ramone had spent the past two months cleaning up. That same bright patch of sun contrasted with the rest of the painting, which was still dull and dirty. It was the real deal.

"What does it mean?" asked Frank. "*How* could we have prevented this?"

"By catching the thief at the museum?" I suggested.

"I don't think so. It's like it's referring to something else—something we should know." He got up from his desk. "Come on."

Frank led the way to the entrance hall table where the mail was stored. Dad was away in Moscow, researching Russian law enforcement techniques for a book, and Mom was preparing for a huge open house this weekend, so the mail had piled up over the past couple of days.

Frank quickly flicked through letters and pulled one out

addressed to Frank and Joe Hardy. He checked the post-mark on the front. "This was delivered yesterday," he said, ripping it open.

I looked over his shoulder as he unfolded a single piece of paper. Sure enough, it was another note made from mismatched letters.

The storm will come, the ship will fail,
The brothers must think, or the art will sail.
The history of old meets technology of new.
To protect the ship, this is your clue.

I looked at Frank in amazement. "And this came yesterday?"

Frank double-checked the postmark. "It sure did. And our mail is always delivered in the morning."

"Then . . . we really *could* have stopped it?"

Frank frowned, rereading the riddle. "I don't know. The riddle's pretty vague, don't you think? I mean, would *you* have known it was talking about the painting?"

I furrowed my eyebrows. "Probably not. At least, not at first. But if we'd read the riddle beforehand, we might have realized what it meant when the tour guide showed us the painting."

"True."

"So what do we do now?" I asked.

"We don't have a choice. We take this to Chief Olaf."

I groaned. "Can't we just leave it in an envelope at the police station?"

Bayport Police Chief Olaf had a bit of a chip on his shoulder about the Hardy boys. I never quite figured out what his problem was, but my guess is it's an insecurity thing. Frank and I had solved more cases in the past few years than he had in his whole life. He seemed to think we were just kids poking our noses into grown-up affairs.

Which, to be fair, we kinda were. But still, we *had* nabbed our share of crooks over the years.

Frank clapped me on the back. "Sorry, bro. Fires? Explosions? This seems like one for the police to handle."

I sighed. "Come on, then. Let's go."

THE PHANTOM 3

FRANK

A HALF HOUR LATER, I RESISTED THE urge to lean over Chief Olaf's shoulders and type the website's address for him. His one-finger typing was driving me insane. I couldn't believe people still typed like that in this day and age!

"This better not be a video about that monkey falling off a tree branch," said Chief Olaf, giving us a stern look from behind his desk.

"It's better than that," said Joe.

"Well, I wouldn't say *better*," I added. "But definitely a lot more serious."

Chief Olaf finally finished typing the address, then moved the mouse to play the video and sat back with a sigh.

Joe and I were sitting on the other side of the desk, but I could tell just by watching his face what parts of the video clip he was watching.

"Is that . . . ?" he began.

"I'm afraid so," said Joe.

The chief's eyes went wide with shock. He watched the whole thirty-second clip, then tore his gaze away to study the letter that had been couriered to us today.

"What does it mean, you could have stopped this?"

Joe and I exchanged looks. This was the bit that was going to be tricky. If Chief Olaf didn't believe us, we were in big trouble.

I handed him the riddle, which he read, frowning. Then he rubbed his forehead.

"I don't get it."

"It's a riddle," said Joe. "Telling us that he was going to steal the painting."

"It arrived at our house yesterday morning," I added. I held up my hands as I saw Chief Olaf inflate with anger, getting ready to scream at us. "But we only saw it this afternoon. Promise."

Chief Olaf regained control of his breathing, which seemed to take considerable effort. He still looked suspicious of us, though.

"Seriously, Chief," I said. "Even if we'd gotten this yesterday, we wouldn't have had a clue as to what it was about. It's just gibberish."

"That it is," Olaf agreed grudgingly. He frowned again. "But why was it sent to you?"

"We have absolutely no idea," replied Joe.

"It's true," I agreed. "Your guess is as good as ours."

"I sincerely doubt that," muttered the chief. "I'll keep hold of these letters," he added, getting to his feet.

"Fine," I said.

Chief Olaf picked up his key ring from the desk and clipped it to his belt. He always carried his keys like that. I'd told him before that it wasn't very secure, but he just waved me away.

"And if you receive any more riddles, bring them straight to me, understand?"

"Understood," said Joe.

He stared at us as if he wasn't sure whether to believe us. Then he jerked his head toward the door. "Get out of here. I've got work to do."

Joe and I quickly left his office and made our way through the police station, emerging into the late-afternoon light.

"What now?" asked Joe.

"Chief Olaf asked a good question," I said.

Joe looked at me in astonishment. "He did? I must have missed that."

"Why was the riddle sent to us?" I said.

"Oh. That one."

I sighed. "You know, we never really got a chance to look around the museum."

"Surely the police did that," said Joe.

"I was watching them. They seemed more concerned with getting statements from us and heading off to lunch than actually looking around."

"It's a crime scene, though," Joe reasoned. "It will be off-limits."

I shook my head. "It can't hurt to check. If it's taped off, we don't go in."

Joe shrugged. "As long as we're done before dinner. I'm starving."

I grinned. "You sound like Chet."

"Hey, the dude has a point," Joe said. "If you've got a high metabolism, you need to keep your energy up, you know?"

"Guess I'll drive, then. Can't have you passing out behind the wheel."

"That's what I love about you, Frank. Always looking out for your little bro."

We arrived at the museum twenty minutes later. It had been reopened, but since it was an hour before closing time, it was pretty much deserted. Joe and I retraced the path our class had taken earlier that day and stopped before the door with the STAFF ONLY sign.

"We're not staff," Joe pointed out.

"No, but we're trying to help. If anyone says anything, we'll just say we got lost."

Joe tried the doorknob. Luckily for us, the door was still

unlocked from earlier. We hurried down the corridor to the restoration room. My hunch was right. There was no crime-scene tape across the door.

I peered inside. Deserted. So the police must have already swept the room for evidence. But there was always a chance they'd missed something.

We searched the room methodically, Joe taking the right side, me the left. We covered the floor slowly, just like our dad had taught us, our eyes moving two inches ahead of our feet, making sure we didn't miss anything.

It took us twenty minutes to cover the room.

"This is hopeless," complained Joe. "There's nothing here."

"I think you're right," I agreed. "Let's check the roof."

We moved along the corridor and through the storage room, then upstairs to the roof. Again, we each took half.

I studied our surroundings before we started. I hadn't noticed earlier, but the roof was covered in a fine layer of dirt and dust. Not surprising, since Bayport hadn't seen rain in a while. And perfect for picking up footprints.

They were everywhere, and most of them seemed to be the heavy-booted imprints of the police from earlier this afternoon. I returned to the door and squatted down, searching for a different impression.

There. A different shoe from the police boots. It looked like some kind of sneaker imprint.

I followed the direction of the sneaker footprints to the spot where the robber had escaped.

I frowned and backtracked. The same set of imprints veered off the path, creating a second trail that headed to a brick structure. I could hear noises coming from inside. The air-conditioning system.

The footprints stopped before the wall. I knew the robber hadn't had time to do this when Joe and I were chasing him. So these prints must have been from earlier, when he was setting up his escape.

But why did he stop here?

I looked up at the brick wall, which was covered in old graffiti tags. Most of them were faded and flaking away, but there was one piece that was new, sprayed over the top of everything else. It was some sort of symbol: a stylistic painting of a half-closed eye.

I leaned in close and sniffed, catching the distinctive smell of spray paint.

"Joe!" I called. "Over here."

He hurried over. "Did you find anything?"

I pointed down. "The robber's footprints stop here." I pointed at the wall. "And that looks fresh."

Joe studied the wall with interest. "You think he did this?"

"I do."

Joe took out his phone and snapped a photo of the symbol. Then he clapped me on the back.

"Good work. First clue of the case."

"Now it's Internet search time," I said.

Joe frowned. "How are we going to do that? It's a picture."

I grinned at Joe. "Keep up with the times, little bro. You can search with images now."

Joe's eyebrows shot up. "Seriously?"

"Come on, Joe. You're too young to get left behind by tech," I teased. "That's Mom and Dad's job."

We arrived back home just as the sun started to sink into the horizon. Mom was lifting groceries from the back of her car as we rolled into the driveway.

"Hello, boys," she said as Joe and I helped her pull the rest of the stuff from the backseat.

"Busy day?" I asked.

She smiled. "Always." She narrowed her eyes and glanced between Joe and me. "Why are you two looking so lively?"

"What do you mean?" I asked, heading toward the back door.

"You know exactly what I mean. You've got that glint in your eye. Just like your father gets when he's working on something."

"We have no idea what you're talking about, Mother," said Joe innocently as we entered the kitchen and dumped the bags on the counter.

"I'll bet you don't," said Mom wryly. "Just be careful, whatever it is you're doing."

"Always," I assured her, giving her a peck on the cheek.

Joe and I hurried to my room, and I booted up my computer. Joe connected his phone to the USB cable, and I transferred the picture he'd taken of the symbol.

"Not bad," said Joe, checking out his handiwork. "I could be a photographer if this whole detective thing falls through."

I rolled my eyes. After I hit the search button, a stream of results flooded the screen.

"Look at that," said Joe proudly. "Imagine how Dad would have done this. He'd have sketched the image, then he'd have to go talk to all his contacts, or search through hundreds of crime records to try and find what he needed to know. While we—"

"While we have to trawl through a list of half a million hits," I finished, scrolling down through the results with a groan.

Most of the results were related to Egyptian hieroglyphs, but I didn't think those were what we were looking for. The eye we had seen was drawn differently, not quite so stylized as the hieroglyphs.

Another big result was the evil eye. The drawing looked similar enough to an evil-eye illustration that I printed out one of the result pages for later, just in case we needed it.

"Can't we narrow the search down a bit?" asked Joe.

"Good idea," I said, adding keywords like theft and burglary.

The search page loaded, and I clicked on the first link.

"Bingo," I whispered.

It was a newspaper report about a series of Bayport-area robberies committed fifteen years ago by a burglar called the

Phantom. This Phantom left the image of the eye as a sort of calling card at each of the crime scenes.

I clicked on another article about a theft committed against some wealthy art collector in New York.

We found more articles along the same lines, each one detailing yet another crime.

"He always seems to hit rich people," Joe observed.

We'd seen that kind of thing before: criminals convincing themselves that they weren't really doing anything wrong, that they were committing "victimless crimes" because those targeted could afford it or were insured.

"I still don't get it," I said, hitting the link to load up the next article. "Why did he send *us* the riddle?"

"Uh . . . maybe that's why," said Joe, pointing at the computer screen.

I looked at the headline.

PRIVATE DETECTIVE FENTON HARDY CATCHES THE PHANTOM

"No way," I said softly, scrolling down to read the article.

Private investigator Fenton Hardy has caught the infamous thief known as the Phantom. Hardy was brought onto the case when the Phantom, responsible for a string of high-profile burglaries, sent a riddle to local police detailing his next crime targeting a local art collector. Hardy cracked the riddle and arrived at the scene, surprising the Phantom mid-robbery.

The Phantom, whose real name is Jack Kruger, is now serving fifteen years in a Bayport correctional facility.

"Go Dad!" cheered Joe.

"Yeah, Dad was hard-core back in the day," I agreed. "But that doesn't help us. If the Phantom really committed these crimes, who's sending us the riddles now? The guy's locked away."

"Maybe not," said Joe. "Check the date."

"Fourteen years ago," I said. "If he behaved himself in prison, he could easily be out on parole."

"And wanting revenge," said Joe darkly.

RIDDLE ME THIS

4

JOE

LEAPED OUT OF BED THE NEXT MORNING. NOT even the prospect of school could kill my mood.

I was excited; I'll admit it. Nothing gets the blood flowing more than a case. I've read the same thing about race car drivers and mountaineers, or anyone who does extreme sports. When they're doing what they love, time loses meaning. They feel alive.

I know that's how Dad felt when he was a PI. I think it's how Frank feels, but he won't admit it. I *know* it's how I feel.

I could smell the aroma of bacon coming from downstairs, so I pulled on a T-shirt and jeans and ran barefoot to the kitchen before Frank could eat it all.

I gave Aunt Trudy a peck on the cheek and slid into my chair across from Frank.

"You try Dad again?" I asked, pouring myself some orange juice. We'd tried calling him yesterday, but it was the middle of the night in Russia.

Frank shook his head. "Thought we'd try after breakfast."

We dug into our food, but before we could finish, there was a knock on the door. I frowned and looked at Frank, my mouth full. "I'll get it," he said.

He came back a minute later, just as I snatched back my fork from where I had been about to commandeer one of his strips of bacon. "Who was it?" inquired Aunt Trudy.

"No one," mumbled Frank. "Wrong address."

"What—" I started to say, but Frank shook his head sharply, and I shut up. Obviously something was going down, but he didn't want Aunt Trudy to know about it.

After we finished our breakfast in record time and were heading to the car, I asked Frank what was going on.

He handed me an envelope.

I turned it over. All it said on the front was Frank and Joe Hardy, written in black Sharpie. No stamp, no address.

"You didn't see anyone?" I asked.

"No one. Clear both ways. He must have had a car."

I opened the envelope and pulled out the now-familiar sheet of paper with words and letters cut from magazines.

Let's play a game. Three nights. Three riddles.
Three robberies. Let's see how clever you really are.
But keep the police out of it unless you want those

closest to you hurt. Chet Morton. Amber Arlington.
Your mother. Your aunt. I know all about your lives.

The Phantom

P.S. As an added incentive, I'll be leaving evidence at the scene of each crime. Evidence pointing to a certain pair of famous detective brothers as the guilty parties. Better get your thinking caps on.

I reread it, fighting down a rising sense of anger. Who did this guy think he was, threatening our family and friends?

"What do you think we should do?" asked Frank.

"Well, we can't tell anyone. He's made it clear what will happen if we do that."

"So that leaves only one option," Frank concluded. "We catch the Phantom ourselves."

I smiled. "I'm going to enjoy this."

"This isn't a game, Joe."

"I know. But when people start threatening those we love, it makes me angry."

"Fair enough." He nodded at the envelope. "There's more in there."

I looked in the envelope to find one more piece of paper. I fished it out and read it.

Big or little
The Masterless Man
Little or big

The Wandering Warrior.
Think two stop me
Think two save them.

"What on earth?"

"Yeah," said Frank as he turned into the parking lot of Bayport High. "He's not exactly making it easy on us, is he?"

"You think we have to crack this by tonight?"

"Three nights. Three robberies. That's what he said."

"We'll just have to see about that," I muttered, staring hard at the riddle.

Classes dragged by as I tried to decipher the riddle. The last two lines kept tripping me up. *Think two stop me. Think two save them.* The Phantom was too smart to misspell "to"; he definitely meant the number two. But it didn't make sense.

I met up with Frank in the cafeteria at lunch. He was already sitting down, and it looked like he'd picked some healthy rabbit food to eat. I shook my head. How was that going to keep him going when we had an infamous thief to catch?

I moved along the line. "Daily special, please," I said.

When I wasn't working on a case, this was my favorite part of the day. It was like Russian roulette with food. You just didn't know what you were going to get.

Today wasn't so bad: french fries and cheeseburgers. I'll take that. Especially over whatever Frank was eating.

I sat down opposite him. He'd placed the riddle in the middle of the table and was staring at it.

"Any luck?" I asked.

He shook his head. "Not yet." He tapped the last lines of the riddle. "This keeps bugging me. 'Think two stop me. Think two save them.' The misspelling has to be intentional."

"My thoughts exactly," I said, shoving a few fries into my mouth.

"So I'm thinking the two is the key. Like, a pair of something."

"Two paintings?" I wondered.

He shook his head. "I don't think the Phantom would repeat himself."

"You don't think *who* would repeat himself?"

I looked up to find Amber and Chet standing by the table with their lunch trays.

I gulped. "Uh . . ." I glanced at Frank. He tried to surreptitiously slide the riddle under the table, but Amber spotted him and grabbed it.

"What's this?" she demanded, taking a seat.

"Nothing," said Frank. "Just some homework."

Chet read the riddle over Amber's shoulder, then frowned at us. "You guys are up to something, aren't you?" He looked around to make sure no one else was listening. "You're working on a mystery."

Amber squealed in delight. "A real-life Hardy boys mystery?"

I looked at her in surprise.

She shrugged. "Come on. Everyone knows about you guys."

Frank and I exchanged a look. "He only said we couldn't tell the police," I pointed out.

"And Dad," added Frank.

"*Who* said?" asked Chet.

"The Phantom," I replied in a low voice.

Chet looked between Frank and me. "I knew it! You guys have another mystery on your hands, don't you?"

Frank nodded. Chet groaned. "Getting involved in this kind of stuff is bad for my health. It's all robbers and men with guns, and chases along cliff-top roads, and . . . and being stuffed inside clocks. It's not good for me."

"So what's this one about?" asked Amber.

Frank sighed and quickly filled Chet and Amber in on everything that had happened since the theft at the museum.

"And this is the next riddle," said Amber excitedly. She read it again and jotted it down in one of her schoolbooks.

"What are you doing?" I asked.

"What does it look like? We can help you with the riddle. Four heads are better than two. Right, Chet?"

Chet let his head drop to the table with a groan.

After school Frank and I decided to head out to the Bayport Correctional Facility. There was still a chance we were wrong that the riddle sender was the Phantom. If he was behind bars, obviously it wasn't him.

"Unless," began Frank as we drove slowly through the

high gates, "he has someone doing his work on the outside. A protégé or something."

"You always have to complicate things," I said with a smile as we parked the car.

Once we were inside the facility's administration building, everything felt subdued. We'd been here before on cases, and I'd hated it.

Frank approached the front desk. "Frank and Joe Hardy to see Jack Kruger."

The official checked a sheet of paper on the desk before him. "You're not on the visitors' list."

"Can you check again?" he asked.

"No need. You're not on the list." The guard frowned. "Who did you say you were visiting?"

"Jack Kruger," Frank repeated.

The guard looked surprised. "Kruger? He was released eight months ago."

"Oh," said Frank. "I see. I don't suppose you have a forwarding address? We're doing a school project on rehabilitation in prison and thought he'd be great to talk to."

The guard shook his head. "Sorry, boys. That's not information I can give out."

"Really?" I said. "Because he's a criminal. Surely it's our right to know where he lives."

The guard leaned on his desk. "First, he's not a criminal anymore. He did his time. And second, *no*, it's not your right. He has a right to privacy. Got it?"

I opened my mouth to argue, but Frank shook his head. I sighed with frustration. It looked like we had no choice but to crack the riddle.

Chet and Amber were waiting outside our house when we got home. I have to say, I didn't mind that much. Amber had been right: Four heads *were* better than two. And a head as pretty as hers . . . well, let's just say I had no complaints if she wanted to hang around.

We gathered in the living room, each with our own copy of the riddle. There was something about one of the lines that was tickling the back of my mind. The Wandering Warrior. I'd heard that phrase before. But where?

"The Masterless Man," said Amber. "Something to do with slavery? An ex-slave?"

"Or an ex-butler," said Frank. "Don't old-fashioned butlers call their bosses Master?"

"What about something to do with a master's degree?" suggested Chet.

"It's the Wandering Warrior I keep going back to," I said. "I'm sure I've heard it before."

"A knight?" suggested Amber.

"A *Jedi* knight?" put in Chet eagerly.

I frowned and leaned back in the chair, closing my eyes to think. The Wandering Warrior. It was familiar, like something I'd seen so often that I didn't even notice it anymore.

I stood up abruptly. "Wait here," I said, and sprinted to my room. I headed straight for the DVDs stacked on my bookcase. I scanned the titles with rising excitement, yanked one out, and hurried back downstairs, holding up the cover for everyone to see.

It was an old kung fu movie called *The Traveling Warrior*.

"That's not the same," Frank pointed out.

My grin faded. "Well, yeah, but it's *similar*."

Frank frowned. "I don't think similar is going to cut it."

"Maybe it's the same idea," said Chet, taking out his phone. He tapped away on the screen for a while, then held it up. "Joe might be onto something." He nodded. "The Wandering Warrior is a term used for a Japanese samurai without a master. They were called *ronin*. These guys would wander around ancient Japan, hiring themselves out as mercenaries."

"You see?" I said excitedly. "'The Masterless Man.' 'The Wandering Warrior.' I was right."

"Fair enough," said Frank. "Can I take a look?"

Chet handed over his phone. Frank scrolled through the entry for a while, then glanced at us. "It says here the *ronin* use a pair of matched swords called *daishō*. The term comes from two separate words, *daitō*, meaning a long sword, and *shōtō*, meaning a short sword."

"'Big or little, little or big,'" said Amber.

"And those last two lines referring to 'two,'" I said. "'Think two stop me, think two save them.' They could refer to the swords! If you stick in a comma, they each make sense. 'Think two, stop me; think two, save them.'"

"So we're talking about a pair of swords from ancient Japan? That's what he's going to steal?" Chet asked.

"No," said Frank grimly. "He's not. Because we're going to stop him."

FINGERPRINTED 5

FRANK

SO WE'D CRACKED THE RIDDLE, BUT OUR next problem was actually finding the *daishō* weapons that the Phantom was planning to steal.

The first thing we did was phone the museum, but they didn't have any Japanese items on display. We tried farther afield, each of us taking towns and cities surrounding Bayport. Some had Japanese exhibits, but none had the ancient weapons the *ronin* used.

After about an hour we gave up. It was evident that the *daishō* were incredibly rare, and every museum we talked to would kill to get their hands on a matched pair.

"So what's next?" asked Chet. He glanced out the window. "It'll be dark soon."

Joe paced back and forth. "If we can't find out where

these swords are, there's nothing we can do. The Phantom wins on the first night. He frames us, and we spend the rest of our lives in jail."

"We won't," I said firmly. "There must be something. . . ." I paused. "I just had a thought."

"Careful now." Joe grinned. "You don't want to overheat your brain."

"What if the swords aren't in a museum? What if they're in a private collection?"

The others stared at me. Then Amber clapped her hands together. "Slow clap for Frank. I think he's got it."

"There's an auction house downtown," Chet informed us. "My mom wanted to buy something but took one look at the opening bids and nearly fainted."

We managed to track down the auction house's phone number.

"Waterson Auctions," answered a cultured British voice after I had punched in the number.

"Uh . . . hi there," I said. "I was wondering if you happened to have any Japanese artifacts going up for auction anytime soon. I'm thinking fifteenth to seventeenth century."

"Ah, you have very refined tastes, sir."

"Thank you," I said, trying to sound sophisticated, as if I spoke to auction houses on a regular basis.

"But I'm afraid we can't help you. With such antiques, we like to perform specialized auctions, focusing entirely on one culture or country. As I'm sure you know, it is very expensive to get ahold of experts to verify and price such items."

"Oh, I'm sure," I said quickly. "In fact, for the last item I purchased from Sotheby's in England, I had to fly in my own expert from Cape Town."

"Really?" said the voice on the other end. "Can I get his number? We're always on the lookout for highly qualified individuals."

"Uh . . . sure," I stammered. "How about I pop in tomorrow with his details?"

"Much appreciated," said the voice. "Is there anything else I can help you with?"

"Actually, yes." I thought I might as well go for broke. "You wouldn't happen to know anyone who might be willing to sell a matched *daishō* set, would you?"

"*Daishō* swords? We sold a set in our last auction, actually."

"When was that?" I asked eagerly.

"Oh, about eighteen months ago now. A local movie producer, I think."

"Do you have his name?"

"I'm sorry. We don't give out personal details on the phone."

"Ah. Of course. Well, thanks for your time." I hung up the phone.

"That was amazing," said Amber. "You should take up acting."

I felt my cheeks flush. "It was nothing."

Joe frowned. "We still don't know who bought the swords."

A quick search on the Internet helped us there. There was only one movie producer in Bayport rich enough to spend that kind of money: a man named James Remington. Apparently he'd worked on a few big-budget Hollywood blockbusters but wanted to settle down permanently in his hometown of Bayport.

Another search gave us his address. It was, unsurprisingly, up in Bayport Heights, where the wealthier set lived.

At half past ten I slipped on my shoes and padded quietly to my bedroom door. Mom was in bed already, and I could hear Aunt Trudy watching television.

I hurried to Joe's room. He was waiting, dressed in all black.

"You ready?" I asked.

He grinned. "I was—"

I held up my hand. "Please, don't say something embarrassing like 'I was born ready.' I'll have to leave you here if you do."

Joe shrugged. "Suit yourself."

He edged past me out the door. "But I was," he said over his shoulder.

We snuck downstairs and out the back door, Joe pausing to grab a bag of chips from the cupboard.

"Seriously?" I asked as we headed into the dark.

"Got to keep my energy up."

We rolled the car out of the driveway so no one would hear us, starting the engine when we were on the street. We stopped to pick up Amber and Chet, then headed toward Bayport Heights. I knew we were close when the houses started to look like fortified mansions and the streets were so clean you could eat your dinner off them. There wasn't a single piece of litter anywhere.

When we arrived at the address, we drove past the house and parked farther down the street.

"How is the Phantom even going to get into the house?" wondered Joe as I killed the engine.

"I have no idea," I said, leaning back to peer through the window. I checked my watch. It was a little after eleven. There didn't seem to be any signs of life inside the house. All the lights were off.

"What if the Phantom's already been here?" asked Amber.

I glanced over my shoulder. "Good point. Maybe we should take a look?"

Joe and Amber nodded. Chet swallowed nervously.

"I suppose," he said. "Although I want it on record that I think this is a bad idea."

We climbed out of the car and hurried along the quiet street. I could hear crickets chirping from a small park off to our left. A dog barked in the distance.

"What if he has dogs?" hissed Chet.

"Good," I said. "It means the Phantom might not get in.

Remember, Chet, we're not here to *steal* the swords. We're here to stop the *Phantom* from stealing them."

"Oh," said Chet. "Yeah. Good point."

The driveway of Remington's house was recessed from the street, flanked on both sides by high walls with ivy growing over the edges. An electric gate blocked the entrance, but that was easy enough to climb.

There was a mailbox sunk into one of the walls. I opened the rear panel and saw it was full of letters. I pulled them out and flicked through them. Bills, junk mail, and one from a travel agency.

"Maybe he's gone on vacation," I whispered.

I put the mail back, and we crept up the driveway toward the house. There was a small set of stairs leading from the driveway to the front door, easily visible from the street. I didn't think the Phantom would get in that way. Too much risk of being seen.

We hurried past the front door and around to the back of the house. A huge garden sprawled into the darkness, its flowers and pruned trees illuminated by concealed lighting.

We moved onto the porch and past the expensive patio furniture. The back entrance was a huge sliding glass door that opened directly into the kitchen.

I hesitated as we drew closer. Either the glass was extremely clean or . . .

"The door's open!" whispered Amber fiercely.

She was right. The patio's sliding door had been pushed open wide enough to admit someone.

"We should call the police!" whispered Chet.

"We've already been through this," hissed Joe. "The Phantom threatened our family. We *can't* call the police."

"Put on your tough-guy face, Chet," I said. "We're catching this guy ourselves."

We entered the kitchen, pausing while our eyes adjusted to the dimness. Outside the kitchen was a long passage that led to the front door, rooms opening to either side. I checked through the first door, a bathroom. Empty. The next door opened into a gaming room. A pool table dominated the space, with old arcade games lining the walls.

The next room was empty, and then we arrived at the room closest to the front door. To our left a set of stairs led up to the second floor.

"Chet and I will look upstairs," whispered Amber.

Joe and I checked the living room. A white leather sofa was positioned in front of a huge flat-screen television.

Joe snapped his fingers. I looked over, and he gestured to the fireplace. On the wall above it was a glass display case.

An *empty* glass display case.

We crept closer. I gently touched the glass, and it swung open. The latch had a digital combination lock attached to it. State-of-the-art stuff, but apparently not enough to stop the Phantom.

"What do we do?" asked Joe.

I shook my head and took out my flashlight. I shone it on the glass case and saw very clear fingerprints. Joe leaned forward to study them.

"You know," he whispered, "I bet the Phantom isn't careless enough to leave his own fingerprints at the scene of the crime."

"I agree," I said.

Joe lifted his index finger and pressed it to the glass next to the print that was already there. I did the same. Then I pulled out my keys and unclipped the little magnifying glass from the key chain.

"You're kidding me," said Joe. "You carry a *magnifying* glass with you?"

"Always be prepared," I said, and we leaned forward to examine the prints.

We spent a while squinting at them in the light of the flashlight. It was hard to be 100 percent sure, but the fingerprint left behind on the display case looked like it could be mine.

"How did he get your print?" asked Joe.

"No idea."

I looked around and spotted a box of tissues. I grabbed a few and wiped down the display case. The Phantom was apparently serious about framing us for this theft.

"There's glass everywhere," remarked Joe. "Our prints could be all over the house."

"Then we've got a lot of wiping to do," I said. "Grab a few tissues and we'll get start—"

I was cut off by a high-pitched scream.

DOUBLE SWORDS

6

JOE

As soon as I heard the scream, I sprinted up the stairs, taking them three at a time. Frank was right behind me.

At the top of the stairs, I heard a whimper to my left. I bolted through the door and into a bedroom, then pulled up short.

Amber stood in the middle of the floor, her hands in the air. A figure dressed in black was behind her, both *daishō* swords in his hands.

They were pointed straight at Amber's neck.

I looked around for Chet, and my heart sank when I saw a dark shadow crumpled on the floor to our left.

I moved toward him.

"Stop!" barked a voice I could only assume belonged to the Phantom.

I pulled up short. "If you've hurt him, I'll make you suffer," I snarled.

"He's fine. Just a knock on the head," growled the masked figure.

I looked at Amber, whose eyes were wide with fear. Razor-sharp sword points rested directly against her skin. Moonlight filtering from the window winked on the blades.

"Take it easy," Frank cautioned, appearing at my side. "No one's going to hurt you."

The Phantom laughed. "I'm perfectly aware of that."

His voice was gruff and low. The Phantom was obviously trying to disguise what he really sounded like.

"So you solved my riddle," he said.

"It wasn't that hard," I replied.

"Then I'll have to make the next one extra difficult."

Frank threw a glare in my direction. The riddle was plenty hard; I just hadn't wanted the Phantom to know that.

"Looks like we've got a bit of a standoff here," I said.

"Not really," said the Phantom. "A standoff would imply that you had something that could hurt me."

"Frank," whispered Amber.

"It's okay, Amber," Frank assured her. "Nothing's going to happen to you."

"You sure about that?" asked the Phantom.

"Yes," said Frank evenly. "Because if it does, we'll make it our life mission to put you behind bars."

The Phantom said nothing. I took the opportunity to look around. The bedroom was minimally furnished. Just the bed and a set of drawers. I checked the walls—

And froze. On the wall to my left was what I thought— and hoped—was a panic button. It was about three arm lengths away.

I licked my lips. What choice did I have? I could see by Amber's stance that she was about to make a move, and I was worried it would lead to her getting hurt. I locked eyes with her and held out my hand in a *wait* gesture. She nodded almost imperceptibly.

I lunged forward and hit the button. Just as I had hoped, the main door alarms were on a separate circuit from the panic button, so even though the Phantom had disabled the alarm system to break in, the panic button still worked. A wailing, shrieking siren erupted around us, echoing through the house.

Amber took advantage of the Phantom's momentary distraction and elbowed him in the stomach. He gasped and staggered back. She ducked away from the blades, and Frank managed to grab her, pulling her toward the door. The Phantom bumped up against the bed. His arms flew out to either side in an attempt to keep his balance, and one of the swords slipped from his hand, slicing through the air directly toward me!

My eyes went wide as I leaned back, trying to dodge the weapon. I bent over, then overbalanced and collapsed onto the carpet. The sword thudded into the wall and hung there for a moment, vibrating.

Then it started to slide back out of the plaster.

I rolled frantically to the side just as it slipped out of the wall and sank point-down into the carpet where my head had just been.

I scrambled to my feet. Frank was rushing toward the Phantom, but the masked figure—still holding one of the swords—rolled off the bed and sprinted toward the window, covering his face and jumping straight into it. The glass exploded and the Phantom followed, disappearing from sight.

Frank and I climbed through the broken window onto a small balcony, where we saw the Phantom clambering over the railing. I leaned over and glimpsed him dropping onto the angled roof of the patio. He hit it with a bang and rolled over the edge before he could stop himself.

I quickly followed him. The metal roof buckled beneath my feet, and for a second I thought it was going to give way. I paused, hands out to balance myself, and shuffled forward.

Moments later I realized my mistake. The roof was steeper than I had thought. My feet started to slide, and I dropped onto my back just as I launched over the edge.

I bent my knees as I hit the grass and rolled to the side. Even so, my breath exploded from my body. I clambered painfully to my feet and staggered around to the front of the house.

I looked both ways. Nothing. But he had to be around here somewhere. He had only been a couple of seconds ahead of me.

I turned in a slow circle, drawing in deep breaths, searching the shadows beneath the streetlights.

There. A movement about three houses down. Someone darting into the shadows.

"You see him?"

I whirled around to find Frank at my side.

"Sure do. Keep up if you can." I set off again, determined to stop the Phantom from escaping with even one of the swords.

I darted into the driveway of the house he had ducked into. The Phantom was struggling to climb a high wall at the far end of the garden. To my surprise, Frank surged past me and leaped up, grabbing hold of the sword's sheath. The Phantom tried to keep hold of it, but I caught up and helped Frank tug it out of his grip.

We both fell onto our backs as the Phantom let go. He pulled himself up onto the wall and turned to face us.

"Hear that?" he said, breathing heavily.

Frank and I slowly got to our feet. I strained my ears, but I couldn't hear anything. I moved my head around slightly.

Sirens.

"You'd better get your friends," the Phantom hissed. "Not sure you'll be able to explain everything to the police."

"If you're talking about our prints on the display case, we wiped them," said Frank.

The Phantom hesitated. I almost smiled. He obviously hadn't expected us to find them.

"Clever," he said. "Just as well that it wasn't the only place I planted them."

Then he turned and dropped into the garden beyond.

Frank and I looked at each other. I knew he was thinking the same as me. We'd both love nothing more than to climb over that wall and chase after the Phantom. But Chet and Amber were still at Remington's place. Chet needed our help, and we had to wipe our fingerprints before the police came. We didn't have time to keep chasing him.

The sirens grew louder. The police couldn't be more than three or four minutes away.

"Come on!" shouted Frank, and sprinted back toward the house. "You get Chet and Amber!" He tossed me the sword as we darted through the patio door.

Frank grabbed a dishcloth from the kitchen and used it to wipe down the glass around the latch. He was making sure the Phantom hadn't planted more of our fingerprints.

I ran up the stairs, almost colliding with Amber at the top. She was dragging Chet out of the bedroom.

I quickly tossed the sword back into the bedroom, then helped her bring Chet none too gently down the stairs, trying to make sure his head didn't bump the wood *too* hard. I could hear the sirens outside as we approached the bottom.

"Help me get him up," I cried. Together, Amber and I managed to heave Chet onto my shoulders. We hurried toward the kitchen.

Frank wasn't there.

"Frank!" I whispered loudly.

He reappeared a moment later. "Just double-checking the living room. I think I cleaned everything."

We slipped into the garden just as the police were nearing the front door. I knew that when they found it locked, they would head to the back. I looked around, then rushed to the wall leading to the next-door neighbor's house. Frank climbed over first, and Amber and I manhandled Chet up after him. He tumbled over the fence.

I hopped up onto the wall and turned back to help Amber, but she was already pulling herself up beside me.

Looking back toward the house, I saw flashlights shining into the back garden. I quickly dropped onto the grass. Amber landed next to me.

"A little help here."

We looked over to find Frank pinned beneath Chet. We rolled his unconscious form over, and Frank pushed himself to his feet. As he did so, Chet groaned.

"Wha—what happened?"

"Shh," whispered Frank. "Keep it down. We're not out of this yet."

Frank was right. He and I crossed the lawn, supporting Chet between us, and snuck around to the front of the neighbor's house. The owners had come out to see what all the commotion was. They were standing out in the street with their backs to us.

We managed to sneak along behind them and head back to where we'd parked the car. After we climbed inside, Frank put it into neutral and released the brake.

We rolled back down the hill until the police and houses were out of sight. Then Frank started the engine, turned us around, and headed back into town.

IDENTITY CRISIS

7

FRANK

THE NEXT DAY WAS SATURDAY, SO JOE and I had the whole day to plan our next move. We'd managed to foil the first of the robberies, but if the Phantom, aka Jack Kruger, kept his word (and there was no reason to think he wouldn't), it meant there would be two more to go. Our best bet to stop him was to find out where he lived and report his whereabouts to the police before he had a chance to follow through on his threats to our family.

I checked the mail first thing, but there were no more riddles—just a flyer for the reopening of the Civil War exhibition at the town hall. So I spent the morning going through Dad's files, hoping to find something that could help us track down the Phantom.

I brought what I found to Joe, who was sitting in the living room, poring over the day's paper.

"Big write-up about the attempted robbery last night," he said.

"Any mention of us?" I asked, placing the folder on the table next to him.

"Nothing."

I felt a surge of relief. "He'll make it harder for us next time."

"Tonight, you mean?" said Joe, putting down the paper and stretching.

Tonight. It seemed crazy that we were waiting on a riddle to foil another robbery that was only hours away.

"What if he doesn't send us a riddle this time?" I wondered.

"He will," said Joe confidently. "He likes this game." He nodded at the file. "What's that?"

"Background on Kruger. Everything I could find on the Internet and from Dad's files."

Joe started leafing through the file while I lay down on the couch and tried to figure out our next move.

"Hey, did you see this?" he called. "Dad kept up his file even after Kruger was put in prison. He mentions Kruger's cell mate here. It says they were released within a few months of each other."

I vaguely remembered seeing something like that in the file, but by that time all the words had started to run together. I nodded, wondering where Joe was going with this.

"It says here that the cell mate was in prison for fraud,

embezzlement, and forgery. Who better to set up a new identity for Kruger than someone who was in prison for that very crime? Someone he shared a cell with for years?"

Joe was right! Kruger wouldn't be careless enough to seek out someone he didn't know. Especially when he already knew someone who could organize a new identity *for* him.

"Is the name in there?"

"Randall Trethaway."

"Address?"

Joe checked the files and nodded. "Dad kept his eye on Trethaway, too. His address is here."

"Then we're in business."

A half hour later I was studying Trethaway's house from the sidewalk. It was a single-story home, white paint peeling from old wooden boards. The windows were covered in wire mesh that was falling away from the frames, and the garden was filled with weeds and cluttered with old newspapers.

"Charming place," muttered Joe sarcastically as we approached the front door.

"I think this is what Mom would call a fixer-upper," I replied, knocking on the door. A tall, bald man answered, wearing neon surf shorts and a vest.

The man said nothing, just looked at us and took a big bite out of an apple.

"Are you Randall Trethaway?" inquired Joe.

Trethaway to be let out of the "deal" he had entered into, and each time Trethaway did his best to convince Kruger/ Brody that this was a good idea. That it would help him to get his story out. Trethaway mentioned movie rights, TV spin-offs, the works.

"Check his sent folder," suggested Joe.

I switched folders and typed in the e-mail address Trethaway was using to communicate with Kruger/Brody, memorizing it as I did so. The search brought up a list of ninety-eight e-mails.

I scrolled back to the first one. If I was hoping for a convenient address and telephone number, I was disappointed. Which made sense. They would have created the fake identity before they started exchanging e-mails using this address.

"Frank!" said Joe urgently. "He's coming back!"

Perfect. I started frantically paging through the e-mails, skimming each one for contact details.

"How much time do I have?" I asked.

"About a minute, I think," he replied.

I frowned and sped up my search even more. Nothing, nothing. Boring. Nothing.

"Thirty seconds!" said Joe. "We gotta go."

"Just a bit longer . . ." There had to be something. Some clue, some—

There.

Trethaway had met up with Kruger/Brody at his place of work.

I noted the address, exited the e-mail program, then closed the laptop. As Joe and I rushed back to the bathroom and were climbing out the window, I noticed a pile of old magazines in the room across the hallway. At that moment I heard Trethaway's keys in the door, and I sprinted around the side of the house, joining Joe as we ran for our car.

CONFUSION 8

JOE

FRANK AND I DECIDED OUR BEST MOVE would be to track down "Stephen Brody" and turn him over to the police. That way, this whole thing could end without anyone getting hurt. We considered telling the police first, but if anything went wrong, the Phantom would be free to carry out his threats against our friends and family. We didn't want to risk that.

His place of business, an auto repair shop and salvage yard, was in an industrial area on the outskirts of town. It was filled with old, rusted car frames and piles of worn tires strewn amid weeds and metal barrels. A heavy pounding came from inside the garage itself. Flashes of blue light illuminated the dim interior as somebody used an arc welder.

Frank nudged me and pointed. Off to the right was a little office partition with glass walls.

Seated behind the desk was Jack Kruger. He looked just like the guy from the article we'd read about Dad catching him; this guy was just a bit grayer around the temples.

Adrenaline rushed through me. Here was the guy who'd been giving us such a hard time—the guy who'd set fire to a priceless painting, who had almost killed me with a sword. The office was the perfect place to confront him; there was nowhere for him to go.

Frank knocked on the door. I tensed, waiting for him to see us and launch into an attack. But all he did was put down the magazine he'd been reading and smile.

"Hi, there. What can I do for you?"

Frank and I glanced at each other uncertainly. This *was* the right guy, wasn't it? It certainly *looked* like the picture of Kruger from the newspaper.

"Mr. Brody?" said Frank.

Kruger got up and came around the desk. He lifted his hand. I tensed, but all he did was hold it out for Frank to shake.

"How can I help you? You got a car that needs fixing?"

"No," I said. "No car. Actually, we're not looking for Mr. Brody."

Kruger looked slightly puzzled. "Then who are you looking for?"

"Jack Kruger," I said.

I watched Kruger carefully as I said his name. I expected anger, fury, a sudden attack. But all I saw was sorrow.

Kruger turned away from us and went back to his desk. "What do you want?" he asked heavily.

"Isn't it obvious?" said Frank.

He nodded. "Money, I suppose. How much?"

Frank shook his head in confusion. "We don't want money."

"Then what? What will it take for you to leave me alone?"

"Hey. We're here to make *you* leave *us* alone," I said.

Kruger stared at us blankly. Finally he shrugged. "Sorry. I have no idea what you're talking about."

I took out the riddle about the samurai swords and dropped it on the table. He leaned forward and studied it, then looked at us quizzically.

"It's a riddle," he said.

"Uh . . . *yeah*," I said. "You sent it to us."

"No, I didn't."

"You did!" I insisted. "You're the Phantom."

"I *was* the Phantom. This"—he waved his hand—"isn't me. Are you boys playing a prank?"

"No, listen. You sent this to us. I'm Joe Hardy, and this is my brother, Frank."

That got his attention. He rose slowly from his chair. "Hardy? As in . . . ?"

"As in Fenton Hardy's sons," Frank explained.

I suddenly realized that Dad was responsible for putting this man away for fifteen years. He was probably going to hold a few grudges about that.

Frank and I exchanged looks, then took a small step back so we weren't up against the desk. But Kruger didn't notice. He hurried around the desk, went straight toward Frank, lifted his arm . . .

. . . and broke into a huge grin.

He gripped Frank's hand and shook it enthusiastically. "Finally I get to meet Fenton's sons! He mentioned you, back when he caught me. Apparently he nearly missed your third birthday, Frank, because he was after me."

"I'm confused," I said. "Why are you so happy to find out who we are?"

Kruger finally released Frank's hand. "Because getting caught was the best thing that ever happened to me. If it wasn't for your father, I'd probably be dead. Please, sit down."

Frank and I took our seats slowly. To be honest, I was wondering if this was some sort of trick, but Kruger sat back down himself and leaned forward on the desk.

"I suppose you're wondering about the name change?" asked Kruger.

Frank nodded. "That and a number of other things."

"Well, I can explain about the first. The thing is, when I was in prison, I realized how wrong I was. I was young when I was the Phantom. I had all these ideas in my head about being a modern-day Robin Hood. Stealing from the rich, that kind of thing."

"Robin Hood gave back to the poor," I pointed out.

"As did I. It was never made known, but I made sizable anonymous donations to various charities. But still, it was wrong. It took your father to show me that. When I got out of prison, I just wanted a fresh start. I knew I couldn't change my name legally. So I went to the one person I knew who could help me."

"Trethaway," said Frank.

"Ah, you've met, have you?" Kruger's face twisted with distaste. "I regret having to go to him, but I had no other choice. He agreed to supply me with a new identity, but only if I'd give him the inside scoop on my life as the Phantom. How I'd planned various heists, that kind of thing. All for this stupid book. I agreed, as long as he kept my new iden- tity secret. Which it looks like he hasn't."

For the first time since we'd been in his office, Kruger looked annoyed.

"So," he continued, "the Phantom has not been sending you riddles. *Or* stealing things. I'm the Phantom. Or, I *was*. And I assure you, it's not me."

"But . . ." I picked up the riddle. "We saw you—him . . . whoever—at the museum, at the house."

"When?"

"Last night and the day before that. Do you have an alibi for those times?"

"I don't. My son saw me early in the evening yesterday, but he went out to a party. The day before that I was home sick. Some twenty-four-hour bug."

Interesting, I thought. He was still claiming his innocence, but he didn't have an alibi. So no matter how much this guy objected, he was probably just trying to bluff us. Question was, what to do about it? Make a citizen's arrest? No proof. Tell the police everything and point them in Kruger's direction? That was a possibility, but I knew they couldn't do anything without proof.

I looked at Frank, but he seemed to be just as lost as I was. He sighed and stood up.

"Okay, Mr. Brody. Thanks for your time." He held a hand out for Kruger to shake.

"Uh, can I rely on your discretion? About my new identity, I mean. I just want to make a fresh start. To get my life back on track."

"Your secret's safe with us."

I looked at Frank in surprise. That was news to me. But I didn't say anything. I shook hands with Kruger, and we left his office.

"What's going on?" I asked Frank as we headed to the car.

"I don't know," he said.

"Wait—you don't actually believe him, do you?" I asked in disbelief.

"I'm not sure," said Frank slowly.

"Come on, Frank! He was just covering. It *has* to be him."

"But he seemed so . . . sincere."

"He'd kinda have to be, Frank. He doesn't want to go back to jail."

"But don't you think he seemed genuinely confused by the riddle? And he didn't recognize us when we walked in. I'm sure of it."

"No. I'm not buying it. He's just a good actor, that's all. Besides, who else could it be if not Kruger?"

"I've been thinking about that," said Frank. "Who stands to profit from the Phantom getting back to work?"

"You mean, besides that man over there," I said, pointing at Kruger's office.

"Yes," said Frank, a slight edge to his voice. "Besides him."

I thought about it. "I give up."

"Maybe someone who's writing a book about the Phantom? Who would see his book probably become a bestseller if the Phantom started up his old tricks again?"

I turned to Frank in amazement. "You think it's Trethaway?"

Frank shrugged. "I saw something when we were climbing out his bathroom window. It didn't click at the time, but looking back . . ."

"What did you see?"

"A pile of old magazines. Like, this high." Frank held his hand above his head.

"Lots of people have piles of old magazines."

"Some of these were lying on the floor. Open."

"So he reads magazines? Big deal."

"Or maybe he cuts them up. To make riddles." He turned to face me. "Think about it. This could only benefit Trethaway. Any controversy will get him free publicity."

"I suppose. You think he's smart enough to do that? Trethaway, I mean?"

"What is it Dad always says? 'If you judge anyone on appearances, you're already five steps behind them.'"

"Then that makes me, like, twenty steps behind," I said. "Because I seriously don't think Trethaway could have done this."

Frank and I climbed into the car. "Regardless, it's an angle we need to look into," he said as he pulled into the road. I glanced over my shoulder as we drove away. Kruger was standing by a repaired car, watching us leave.

I saw it instantly as we drew up to our house. An envelope lying on the steps.

I got out of the car and hurried over. It was the same style of envelope, the same writing. I picked it up and pulled out the sheet of paper as Frank joined me.

Of
18
16
By
61
12

For
750,000
11 o'

I blinked, then looked at Frank. "And now? Is this a riddle?"

"Must be."

"And he expects us to crack this before tonight?"

"Looks like it." Frank sighed. "Call Chet and Amber. Ask them to meet us at the Meet Locker. I think we'll need some help with this."

CAUGHT IN THE ACT

9

FRANK

CHET AND AMBER WERE ALREADY WAITING at the Locker, Chet tucking into a burger and fries while Amber searched the Internet for clues.

"Anything?" I asked, slipping into the booth next to her.

She shifted over to give me room. "Not yet. There doesn't seem to be any pattern. It just looks like random numbers."

"Except for the last line," Joe pointed out. "That's obviously the time we need to solve it by."

I checked the last line. *11 o'.* Short for eleven o'clock. Fair enough. One point to Joe.

"Okay," I said, "let's break it down."

Joe studied the piece of paper. "There *is* kind of a pattern.

Each pair of numbers is preceded by a word. Of 18–16. By 61–12. For 750,000–11 o'."

"Could they be referring to biblical passages?" asked Chet around a mouthful of fries.

The waitress approached while Amber checked her laptop. I ordered a chocolate shake and Joe ordered a club sandwich.

"I don't think so," Amber said eventually. "I mean, they *could* be. But there's an 18–16 in the books of Proverbs, Luke, Revelation, Exodus . . . pretty much *all* of them."

"Probably not that," I said.

"Combination locks?" suggested Amber.

"To what?" asked Joe.

"Safes? Do safety-deposit boxes have codes?" she said.

I shook my head. "No. Keys."

"Map coordinates," said Joe, sitting upright suddenly.

I looked at the numbers again. It was a possibility.

Amber broke the numbers into map coordinates. 18:1:6.611 latitude and -2:7:50.000 longitude. She entered them into a mapping program, but nothing came up.

This was getting frustrating. I stared at the piece of paper. There was something familiar about the words. *Of, by,* and *for.* Where had I heard that before?

The waitress brought my shake and Joe's sandwich. He took a bite, then said thoughtfully, "What about an anagram? The words?"

We spent the next few minutes rearranging *of*, *by*, and *for*, but we didn't come up with anything helpful. Then we added up the first two sets of numbers, getting 34 and 73, but again, there was nothing we could *do* with the numbers.

It was already after four, and we were no closer to solving the puzzle.

"What about Dad?" Joe suggested.

"What about him?"

"Can't we phone him? Ask him if he can help?"

"The Phantom said not to tell the police *or* Dad. It's not worth the risk of endangering Mom. Or Aunt Trudy."

By this time we had all finished our food and sat in dejected silence, staring at the riddle lying in front of us. Joe pulled some cash out of his wallet and dropped it on the table where the waitress had left the check. The top note was a five-dollar bill; Abraham Lincoln's face stared at me.

Amber reached over to collect the money. But before she did, I slapped my hand down on the notes.

Honest Abe. Sixteenth president of the USA. I grabbed the pen from the table and drew a line through the number 16 on the paper.

"Of the people, by the people, for the people," I said.

Chet stared at me as if I was nuts. But Joe and Amber looked at me with expressions of dawning realization.

"The Gettysburg Address," said Joe.

I looked at the last three numbers: 18, 61, and 12.

"Quick—the date—the exact date the Civil War began."

Amber typed into her laptop. "April 12, 1861," she answered.

That just left 750,000. "Are you on the wiki page?"

Amber nodded.

"How many people died again?"

"Seven hundred fifty thousand," said Amber in an awed voice.

We all stared at one another, then down at the sheet of paper. We'd cracked the code!

"I still don't get it," said Chet. "The Civil War, sure. But what's going to get stolen?"

I opened my mouth, then snapped it shut again. He was right. We still didn't know the target.

"It must be something to do with Lincoln?" asked Chet.

"No," said Amber. "This is all about the Civil War. Not Lincoln."

"Was there anything at the museum?" I asked.

Joe shook his head. "Not that I saw."

Something rang a bell in my mind. The flyer that came in the mail. The Civil War exhibition reopening at the town hall!

"The Civil War exhibition!" I gasped. "We got a flyer in the mail! It's been reopened in the town hall. All the stuff went away to be cleaned and restored."

"Yeah, but the town hall is right outside the police

station," said Joe doubtfully. "He wouldn't be that stupid."

I shook my head. "I think *that's* where the Phantom is going to strike. At eleven o'clock tonight."

At nine o'clock, Joe and I were sitting in our car a few houses down from Trethaway's place.

This time we had a plan. We still weren't sure if the Phantom was Trethaway or Kruger or someone else entirely. My money was on Trethaway, but Joe was still stuck on Kruger.

We had split into two groups. Amber and Chet had staked out Kruger's workplace and followed him home. They were watching his house, while Joe and I took Trethaway's. All of us had video cameras. This time our aim was to get solid evidence of the theft.

Joe checked the battery in his video camera and switched it to night-vision mode. "Want to place a bet?" he asked.

"On?"

"On whether it's Trethaway or Kruger."

"Sure. Ten bucks?"

"Come on. Put your money where your mouth is, bro. Twenty."

I held out my hand. "Deal."

About an hour later we saw Trethaway's door open, and the man himself stepped outside. I leaned forward, and Joe focused the camera on him.

He was wearing dark clothes—perfect for breaking and

entering. He looked both ways down the street, then jogged to his car, slid behind the wheel, and drove off with a little spin of his tires.

"He's in a hurry," I pointed out, checking the rearview mirror before setting off after him. "Looks like you might owe me twenty bucks."

I kept my distance as we tailed Trethaway through the city streets. There was enough late-night traffic that even if he had looked in his mirrors, he wouldn't have noticed we were following him.

Still filming, Joe picked up the two-way radio we were using to stay in touch with Chet and Amber.

"Guys? Any movement on your side?"

There was a hiss and crackle, and then Chet's tinny voice echoed through the car. "Delta One, remember?"

"Huh?" said Joe.

"Use the proper code names. Delta One and Delta Two. Come on. You gotta do this properly."

Joe rolled his eyes at me. "Fine. Delta Two to Delta One. Come in, Delta One."

"Delta One here. No movement in target's house. Everything dark."

I frowned. "Everything dark? Not even a single light?"

"No, no lights on at all. Looks like nobody's at home."

That was a bit worrisome. Why would Kruger be out at this time? Unless he was asleep already?

I gestured for Joe to hand over the radio as I eased to

a stop at a traffic light. Trethaway had made it through before the light turned red, but I could still see him up ahead.

"Guys, do me a favor and go knock on his door. Make it loud. We need to know if he's in there or not."

Amber's voice came over the speaker. "Sure. Give us a couple of minutes."

I handed the radio back. The light had turned green, so I hit the gas and headed off to find our target.

Only problem was, he had disappeared.

I slowed down, searching the road ahead, checking the cars parked along the sidewalk. Joe was staring out the passenger window, trying to see if he had pulled off onto any side streets.

"You think he saw us?" he asked.

"Nah. We weren't tailing him too closely."

"Yeah, but what if he's paranoid?" Joe said. "He was in prison for a while."

I hadn't thought of that. Up ahead, a police car pulled out of a gas station and passed us, heading in the opposite direction. It disappeared into the darkness.

A second later I heard the squeal of tires and Trethaway's car skidded into view, sliding onto the main street from a side alley. His car sped off into the distance, then skidded around yet another corner, vanishing from sight.

"After him!" shouted Joe.

I stomped on the gas and gunned the engine. I could

see his taillights up ahead, swerving from side to side as he fought to keep control of his car.

"You think he spotted us?" I shouted.

"I think the cops spooked him," said Joe. "Looks like I might owe you that twenty bucks after all."

Trethaway took us on a chase away from the city's center, moving through smaller suburban streets. Our cars skidded around corners, spinning along the asphalt as we played cat and mouse through the narrow streets.

I managed to keep him in sight, but I didn't know what to do. We couldn't ram him off the road. And this was getting dangerous.

Finally Trethaway screeched around a corner and mounted the sidewalk, ramping his car over the curb and into somebody's garden. He kept going, pulling up the grass as he shot out the other side and back onto the street. Sparks flew as his undercarriage scraped the road, but he didn't slow down. In fact, he put on another burst of speed, zigzagging across the road as he tried to lose us.

I sighed and slowed down, pulling over to the side of the street.

"What are you doing?" shouted Joe. "He's getting away!"

"It's too dangerous," I said. "What if someone had been out walking their dog? Trethaway could have hit them!"

Joe punched the dashboard in frustration. I held up a calming hand.

"Relax. We lost him, but if he *is* the Phantom, then we

know where he's going to be in an hour, remember?"

Joe's frown turned into a grin. "Oh yeah! I forgot about that."

I headed back toward the center of Bayport. We hadn't quite reached the town hall when our radio crackled to life.

"Delta Two, this is Delta One. The worm has flown the coop. Repeat, the worm has flown the coop."

Joe lifted the radio. "What does that even mean?"

Amber's voice came from the speaker. "It means he was not at his house. Repeat, he's not there. We looked in all the windows. The house is deserted."

Joe and I glanced at each other in amazement.

"There's more," said Amber. "We're outside the town hall. I think we just saw movement inside."

Chet's excited voice came from the speaker. "Looks like he's early!"

RADIO SILENCE

10

JOE

WE PARKED TWO BLOCKS AWAY from the town hall. Best not to have our car on any surveillance cameras, just in case anything went wrong.

I pulled out a face mask and handed it to Frank. He held it up and examined it.

"Freddy Krueger?" he asked.

"I thought it suited you."

"What did you pick for yourself?" he asked.

I held up a clown mask. But no ordinary clown mask; this one had demonic eyes and sharp yellow teeth.

"I think I'll stick with Freddy."

Frank started to pull on the mask as I looked at him in amazement.

"What?" he said.

"Seriously? We're going to walk two whole blocks with these masks on? It's not Halloween. It will look suspicious."

Frank flushed slightly and stuffed the mask in his pocket. "Good point. Let's go!"

The streets were damp from an early evening shower. The streetlights reflected in the puddles as we headed toward the gabled roof of the town hall, easily visible over the surrounding buildings.

My two-way radio crackled to life.

"Delta Two, come in."

I glanced around to make sure no one was watching. "Delta Two. Where are you?"

"Rear entrance. The town hall door's been cracked open."

We jogged along the street that led to the town hall. The building was fronted by a large square of grass that was used for pet shows and art fairs.

But directly opposite the town hall, on the other side of the street, was Bayport police headquarters. I could see cops from here, walking into the station and heading out into squad cars to start their evening patrols.

I felt my stomach do a little somersault. "Frank, this is crazy. If we get caught, there's no way to prove we're not trying to steal anything."

"I know," Frank said grimly. "But we can't let this creep get away with another theft. If we don't stop him, who will?"

I couldn't argue there. Dad had taught us to do the right

thing no matter what—and this definitely qualified.

I glanced up at the town hall as we skirted around the side of the redbrick building. Five floors, all windows dark. We found Amber and Chet waiting in the back.

We were all dressed in black, but whereas Chet, Frank, and I looked like troublemakers, Amber looked like she'd stepped off a movie set. She wore a charcoal-gray hoodie over her black shirt, but she somehow managed to make it seem cool.

"We parked a couple of blocks away," Frank told them as I pulled the last two masks from my pockets.

"Dracula or Frankenstein?" I asked. "Sorry, it's all the store had left."

"Dracula! Cool!" whispered Amber, snatching the Dracula mask even as Chet was starting to make a grab for it. "Sorry, Chet," she said. "You snooze, you lose. Hey, do we get to keep the masks?"

"Uh . . . sure. All yours."

"Awesome!" Amber pulled on her mask. "I vant to suck your blood!" she whispered, hands raised into claws as she turned toward Chet.

"Hey, cut that out," said Chet, skipping out of reach. He put on the Frankenstein mask while Frank and I did the same with ours.

"Okay," said Frank. "Everyone ready? Joe, you have the camera?"

I patted my pocket.

"Good. Let's go."

I took out the camera and flicked open the LCD panel. The screen lit up with a green phosphorescence as the night vision picked out the others heading into the town hall. I focused the camera down at the door's lock as I passed. The wood around the edge was splintered. It had clearly been forced open—which meant the Phantom must have disbanded the alarm system already. I felt a twinge of annoyance. He had said eleven o'clock. How were we supposed to catch him if he didn't play by his own rules?

Which, I supposed, was the whole point. It wasn't as if he *wanted* to get caught, no matter how much of a game he thought this was.

The back door opened into a kitchen with two huge ovens and a few industrial fridges. The kitchen led into a dark hall with offices on either side. I could see light up ahead, filtering in through the front windows of the building.

We crept forward, stopping before we arrived at the entrance hall. The building actually used to be an old house, some kind of mansion built by the founder of Bayport in the eighteenth century, so it was big and creaky.

We waited and listened. I used the camera to get a good look into the entrance hall, using it like I would night-vision goggles. I took in wooden floorboards, an information wall showcasing the sights of Bayport, tables with flyers on them, a little kiosk where the receptionist worked, and a flight of stairs leading up to the next floor.

After a minute or so, Frank led the way into the entrance hall. We moved slowly to the stairs.

"Walk close to the wall," Frank hissed. "Less chance of the stairs creaking there."

My brother the professional burglar. I'd have to ask him how he knew that.

I pointed the camera at the second floor, just to make sure the Phantom wasn't standing in the dark, watching us. But nobody was there. We started climbing.

"Hey," whispered Amber. "What floor is this Civil War display on?"

Frank paused and looked at me. I shrugged. Amber shook her head and headed back down the stairs. I watched over the banister as she used a small flashlight to scan the notice board and the flyers. Then she hurried back to join us.

"Top floor," she said.

We crept up the stairs, pausing at every floor to listen. I have to admit, it was more than a little creepy. I know the Phantom was supposed to be good, but I couldn't hear a single sound that seemed out of place.

When we arrived at the top floor, I saw that the passage led both left and right. I counted the doors. Ten. The exhibit could be behind any one of them.

Frank put his ear against the wood of the first door. He listened for a moment, then shook his head and moved to the next one. I was going to ask why he didn't just open the door to check, but then I realized that in this silence, the noise of the door latch would sound like an explosion.

We checked each door, but there wasn't a sound behind any of them. Frank leaned in close to whisper. "We're going to have to open the doors to check out each room. Chet, you and Amber wait at the bottom of the stairs in case he's hiding somewhere else."

"Uh, what are you going to do?" asked Chet.

"Try and tackle him before he gets out of the room."

"Good luck," whispered Amber.

They tiptoed down the stairs, and Frank and I moved along the passage.

"The study would most likely be at the end of the corridor," I noted softly. "A study usually has a view of some kind."

"Good point," said Frank.

We tiptoed across the carpeted hall to the last door. We were only halfway there when my radio crackled to life.

"In position," said Chet. "Ready to grab any Civil War treasures that come our way."

Frank winced and lifted the radio to his lips. "Radio silence, please," he whispered.

When we arrived at the door, Frank put a hand on the handle and looked at me. I nodded, and he started to open it.

But he didn't get the chance.

"*This is the police,*" blared a loud voice. "*Identify yourselves!*"

ROOFTOP RACE
11

FRANK

I WHIRLED AROUND IN SHOCK. JOE STARED AT me with wide eyes.

"I repeat, whoever is in the town hall, identify yourselves."

Our eyes dragged down to our radios, where the voice was coming from. And it was the unmistakable voice of Chief Olaf.

"And if you're going to rob the town hall, in the future, use a secure connection. Your chitchat is coming through every police radio in the station."

I quickly put my radio to my mouth. "Delta One. Abort. Repeat: Abort."

From the other side of the door came a terrific crash and the sound of shattering glass.

I pushed the door open and saw a dark figure scrambling out the window. He turned on the windowsill and reached up, then pulled himself onto the roof. I ran forward to try and grab his legs, but he yanked them from my grip.

My eyes were drawn to movement across the street. Police officers were pouring from the station, running toward the town hall, flashlights bobbing and weaving, cutting through the night. They were already more than halfway across the front lawn. There was no way Joe and I were getting out the traditional way.

Besides, we had a robber to catch.

I turned around and reached up to the roof. My fingers caught hold of the gutter, which I yanked on to test its strength. It held. I pulled myself up onto the roof and moved aside so Joe could join me. I kept low, hoping the police wouldn't see my silhouette from below. The sky was still cloudy, so we were in luck.

I scanned the rooftop and saw the Phantom to our right. He was taking his time. Joe and I set off after him, and I immediately understood his caution. The roof's shingles were slippery from the earlier rain. One wrong move and we would go sliding down five stories to the hard ground below.

We picked our way across as fast as we could. I glanced over my shoulder to check on the police. I turned away for only a second, but as soon as I did, I felt something slip underfoot, as if I were sliding on ice. I looked down in horror and saw that an entire shingle had come off, sliding down the angled roof with my foot still on it.

I lost my balance and fell on my back, hitting the shingles with a terrific crash. I felt some of them shatter beneath my elbow. I started to slide amid an avalanche of red shingles, heading straight for the edge. My arms flailed behind me, frantically reaching for anything to grab hold of. I tried to twist around, but the shingles shifted beneath me so much that I was now heading for the edge headfirst. I opened my mouth to shout for help—

And lurched to a stop. My eyes swiveled up to see Joe lying stretched out full length, his feet hooked over the peak of the roof and one hand gripping my ankle.

The shingles flew past me. I heard them crash to the ground, shattering the quiet with loud cracks. I struggled to look over my shoulder. The police had stopped running and had turned their attention to the roof.

I reached up and grabbed Joe's arm. He had shifted to the side slightly, where the rooftop was still in one piece. He let go of my ankle, and I crawled up toward him.

A shout from below informed me that we'd been spotted. Nothing to be done about that now. Joe moved back up the roof and stood up. I followed his example, my legs a bit shaky, and we set off again.

The Phantom was at the opposite edge of the roof by now, and as we watched, he dropped from sight. I wondered if he had another bungee cord or if there was some other way down. I really hoped that whatever it was, we could use it too.

Just then I heard a shout behind us. I glanced back and saw Chief Olaf peering over the edge of the roof. He looked around, then ducked back inside the building.

I smiled. There was no way he would come up here after us. He'd send some of the younger officers.

My face was dripping with sweat, my breathing amplified by the mask. The sweat was getting into my eyes, stinging them, and I couldn't even wipe it away. I couldn't risk lifting the mask in case we were being watched.

We reached the end of the roof, and I breathed a sigh of relief. Just below us, attached to an emergency door on the fifth floor, was a fire escape.

But as we watched, the same door started to open.

Joe and I did the exact same thing. Without a moment's hesitation we leaped off the roof, dropping onto the fire escape with a loud clang. We rammed ourselves up against the door, slamming it shut again. Someone on the other side pushed against it, but the two of us had more weight. The only problem was, we couldn't just stand there all night. The police would be coming around the side of the building any moment now.

I looked at Joe. "We have to make a run for it."

He nodded. "When you're ready."

"Let's go."

We jerked away from the door and clattered down the

series of fire-escape ladders leading to the ground. Each time we hit a metal landing I would shove the ladder back up again and push the latch into place. It wouldn't stop anyone, but it might give us an extra minute or two.

We landed on the street behind the town hall just as the Phantom was sprinting away, heading away from the police station. We set off after him, putting our athletic prowess to good use.

Just as we started to catch up with him, we heard more sirens blaring, closer this time.

I looked over my shoulder and saw two squad cars screech around a corner. Joe grabbed me and we ducked into a narrow alley, leaving the Phantom in clear view.

The squad cars shot past us. We moved deeper into the alley, emerging one block over. Now we were on the same street we had used to get to the town hall in the first place. That meant our parked car wasn't far away. If only we could get to it.

More sirens. We ducked back into the alley, hunkering down in the shadows as they sped past.

"You think they'll catch him?" asked Joe.

"I doubt it. He's too slippery. Speaking of which . . ." I pulled off my mask and stuffed it into my backpack, wiping the sweat from my face.

"You think this is a good idea?" asked Joe, taking his off as well.

"Better than getting caught wearing them. At least like this we can come up with an excuse if we need to."

My phone beeped, indicating an incoming message. It was a text from Amber.

EVERYTHING OK? WE MADE IT OUT. DROPPING CHET OFF AND HEADING HOME.

I quickly texted back. SO FAR SO GOOD. THE LOCKER @ 11 A.M.?

SEE YOU THEN.

"Chet and Amber are clear," I said, putting my phone away.

Joe breathed a sigh of relief. "One less thing to worry about."

"Let's get back to the car," I said. I peered out of the alley and saw that the street was deserted. We slipped out and headed along the sidewalk. I wasn't sure if we should run as fast as we could or just walk calmly. Running meant we got away faster, but if we were caught, it would look suspicious. Walking meant it took us longer and there was more chance of being discovered, but if that *did* happen, we could try and talk our way out of it.

We couldn't even dump our masks, because our DNA was all over them. I wasn't sure if the Bayport police had DNA profiling kits, but better to be safe than sorry.

We heard sirens a few streets over as we turned onto the road where we had left our car. It was still there, and even better, there were no police waiting for us.

I climbed behind the wheel and rolled down the window. The sirens were coming from the east, so I started the engine and headed west.

"Where are you going?" asked Joe after a while. "Home's the other way."

"We're not going home."

Half an hour later, I hopped out of the car and knocked on Trethaway's door. Nothing. I knocked harder, but there was no answer. I headed around the back and tested the window Joe had opened yesterday.

"What are you doing?" asked Joe, now standing behind me.

"Looking for evidence. And if I don't find that, waiting for Trethaway to get back."

"Are you serious?"

I paused and looked back at Joe. "Yes. I'm tired of all these games. Our families have been threatened, we almost got busted by the police tonight, I nearly fell off the roof, and who *knows* what he stole from the museum. I want this finished before *he* decides it's over. Which means we have to do it tonight. Tomorrow is the last riddle, remember?"

I climbed through the window and headed into the bedroom, where the pile of magazines still sat. I picked up a few of them, but I couldn't see any that had words and letters cut out.

Next I went for the computer while Joe hung around the front door, shifting from foot to foot.

"I don't like this," he said. "If you're so sure it's him, we should call the police. Maybe they've already caught him!"

"We can't call the police. If they haven't caught him, he's

still free to carry out his threats. We'll wait here and confront him when he comes home."

Then I heard an ominous click, like a gun being cocked.

"Confront me about what?" growled Trethaway.

I looked up and saw that Joe had stiffened. Trethaway
was standing behind him, and from the look of it, he had a
gun shoved up against Joe's back.

THE FINAL COUNTDOWN
12

JOE

TRETHAWAY PRODDED ME IN THE BACK with what felt like a pistol. "Next to your brother," he said.

I moved to stand next to Frank and turned around. The living room was still dark, but Trethaway reached out and flicked the light switch. He stared at us curiously.

"What are you doing in my house?" he asked. "I don't have anything to steal."

"We're not here to steal from you!" I protested.

"No? Then you won't mind if I call the cops?" He reached into his jacket, and that was when I saw that he wasn't holding a gun at all, but a small cardboard tube of what looked like . . .

Candy? I'd seriously thought a cardboard tube was a gun? In my defense, the candy tube was about the same circumference.

Trethaway upended the tube into his mouth. He tossed it onto the couch and took out his cell phone, crunching away while he studied us.

"Seriously. What do you want?"

"Like you don't know," I said.

"No. I don't."

"Where were you tonight?" Frank demanded.

"The movies. Late show."

"Hah. A likely story," said Frank. "Any proof?"

Trethaway fished in his pocket and pulled out a ticket stub. He handed it over and I inspected it. It was dated today. And it was for the ten p.m. show.

"That means nothing. You could have bought the ticket as an alibi and slipped out again."

"An alibi for *what*?"

"For impersonating the Phantom and stealing from the Civil War exhibit at Bayport's town hall."

Trethaway's eyes grew wide. "Seriously? Kruger's at it again? This is great! Well . . . *obviously*, not great. But great for my book! What did he steal? Has there been more than one robbery? Why isn't it in the news?"

He ran over to his desk and scrambled around for a notepad and pencil.

"Uh, Frank?" I said.

"Yes, Joe?"

I held out my hand. Frank sighed and fished around in his pocket until he found a ten-dollar bill.

"I'll owe you the rest," he said, handing it over.

"Don't feel so bad. At least we know it has to be Kruger now."

I woke up the next day ready to take on the world. Well, to take on Kruger, at any rate.

The first thing I did was check the mail. No riddle. Which was a bit worrisome, because this was the final day. If we didn't catch the Phantom in the act tonight, we'd *never* catch him.

Frank was already up. He had the car keys in his hand when I entered the kitchen to grab some breakfast.

"Ready?" he asked.

"For breakfast? Always."

"No. To go see Kruger."

"Now?"

"Now."

"But—"

"Come on, Joe. We don't have much time."

I sighed, then grabbed a couple of apples from the fruit bowl, and we headed out to the car.

Sunday traffic was light; it didn't take us long to get to Kruger's. His home wasn't anything impressive. A small, one-story house with a neatly trimmed yard. It looked deserted.

"You think he's flown the coop?"

"No," said Frank. "Still one more riddle. One thing I've learned over the past couple of days is that this guy has an ego. He won't leave without finishing what he started."

As we sat there, an old pickup truck pulled up. It was Kruger. He got out and stretched.

We hurried across the street. Kruger saw us coming and, I have to say, did *not* look happy.

"Boys," he said, "I'm in a bit of a hurry. Have to drop some parts off at the shop."

"On a Sunday?" I asked.

"Need them for tomorrow. Rush repair job. I had to head out of town yesterday to get the parts."

"Wait," said Frank. "You're saying you've been out of town?"

"Uh . . . yeah."

"Last night, too?"

"Yes!"

"Where?" I asked.

"Why?" he demanded.

"We're curious," said Frank.

Kruger sighed. "Last night I was about two hundred miles away. Sleeping in a horrible motel, if you must know."

"Can you prove it?" I asked.

"Why should I?"

"Please, sir," said Frank. "Just do this for us and we'll leave you alone."

Kruger muttered something I couldn't hear and fished around in his wallet. He pulled out a piece of paper and handed it to me.

"I'll do it since you're Fenton's sons. This is a receipt from the motel, so I can claim expenses."

I studied the receipt, then handed it to Frank.

"Sir," he said. "We're really sorry. We . . . we messed up."

"Can I go now? I'm tired."

"Of course." Frank handed back the receipt, and we both hurried back to the car.

We sat in our seats and stared out the window at Kruger. There was movement inside as someone—a guy who looked to be a few years older than Frank—flicked back a curtain to see who was outside. Kruger waved up at the window, and the boy waved back. I figured it must be his son, the one he'd mentioned when we first interviewed him.

"So . . . ," Frank began.

"Both have alibis," I said.

"Yup."

"Which means we're no closer to knowing who it is than we were yesterday."

"Yup," said Frank.

I pulled the ten-dollar bill out of my pocket and gave it back to Frank. "Better hold on to this then."

Frank took the money and started the car. "Where to?"

"Home. I want a proper breakfast, and then I need to sit down and think this case through."

"Me too," said Frank with a sigh.

No chance of that, though. As we pulled into the driveway, both of us saw an envelope sticking out of the mailbox.

"Here we go again," I muttered, running to grab it while Frank drove the car into the garage.

When he joined me, I tore the envelope open. It was two pages long this time. The first was a note to us, made once again from letters and words clipped from magazines and newspapers.

Tick-tock, boys. Midnight tonight is the time. See you there?

I turned to the next page. It was filled edge to edge, top to bottom, with the numbers one and zero handwritten over and over again in random patterns.

I turned it over. Nothing on the back.

Frank took it from me. "This looks like binary code," he said. "It's used in computing to encode instructions."

"Can you read it?"

Frank laughed. "No."

"So what are we supposed to do with it?"

Frank tapped the paper to his chin. "Maybe we scan it into a JPEG, then use text recognition to turn the scan into actual numbers again?"

"And then?"

"Then we search on the Internet for what those numbers mean," he said, hurrying through the door.

"Okay. Sounds like you know what you're doing."

Frank already had the letter in the scanner by the time I got to his room. We waited while the scanner buzzed and whined. Then the numbers flickered to life on Frank's monitor.

"Now what?" I asked.

"Now I search for a handwriting recognition website."

I flopped onto his bed and leafed through a graphic novel. I knew from past experience it was best to let Frank do his thing with computers. He tended to get irritated if I hovered at his shoulder.

"Done," he announced about ten minutes later. "I ran the scan through a website, and it sent me a Word file."

"And what's next, O Wise One?"

"Now I copy and paste the binary numbers into a converter."

"And you've managed to find a binary converter?"

Frank looked at me. "Binary isn't some kind of rare, magical language. It's computer code. Pretty well known."

"If you say so."

Frank returned to his work. After a minute I heard a sigh of frustration.

"It's just gibberish! There's no meaning here."

I glanced at the screen. The converter had turned the ones and zeros into a series of meaningless letters and numbers. We sat there and scanned each line, but there wasn't anything that made sense.

"So much for that," said Frank.

My phone rang. "Hey, Amber."

"Hi, Joe. We still on for the Locker at eleven?"

"Yep. We got another clue this morning—a page filled with ones and zeros."

"Oh, you mean binary?"

"Uh, yeah. Binary." I turned away from Frank. "That was my first thought too."

I heard Frank snort behind me.

"So have you translated it?"

"We tried. It's just nonsense. Random letters and numbers."

"Well, send it to me. Chet, too. Four heads are better than two, remember?"

I smiled. "Sure, we'll send it over." I turned around, but Frank had already e-mailed it. "It's on its way to you now."

"Thanks. See you at eleven. We'll compare notes."

After I had hung up the phone, I examined the physical letter. I had a feeling we didn't need all the fancy stuff Frank was doing. Surely the puzzle had to be solvable from this single piece of paper?

"Can we somehow add the numbers up? Maybe each line? Then each line might correspond to a letter of the alphabet?"

Frank grinned at me. "Isn't that the code we used when we were six years old?"

I nodded. "You never know."

Frank spent the next twenty minutes adding the numbers on each line, then using that number to pick a letter of the alphabet. When he had finished he turned to me in amazement. "By Jove, I think you cracked it!"

"Really?"

"No." He handed me the paper he'd been writing on, which read, *fhdiosfnsoortndangnvangopapqnvcncnspavvgngoo*.

"Maybe it's a Scandinavian work of art."

"That's exactly what it's not. Nice try, though."

He turned back to the screen. I grabbed a blue tack from his desk and stuck the riddle on the wall. I paced, staring at it, trying to figure out what it could mean.

An hour later Chet and Amber both e-mailed to say they had come up with nothing.

"I'm going to the kitchen," I said with a yawn. "Want anything?"

"Orange juice," said Frank absently, not taking his eyes from the screen.

I headed downstairs and made myself a sandwich. Then I poured two glasses of orange juice, balanced one on my plate, grabbed the other in my free hand, and climbed back up the stairs.

Frank's room was at the far end of the hall, so I could see into it as soon as I hit the landing. As I approached, my eyes fixed on the riddle stuck on the wall.

I stumbled to a stop. I blinked, moved back a few steps, then forward again, making sure I wasn't seeing things.

"Frank," I said, carefully putting down the food and drinks. "Look."

"You okay?" he asked, and stood up. "You look weird."

"Turn around," I said calmly, "and look at your wall."

Frank did so, and when he gasped in surprise, I knew he'd seen what I had seen.

The riddle—the puzzle made up of ones and zeros—was actually a picture!

The ones and zeros imitated shading in the image, but the pattern they formed could only be seen from afar.

And the picture Frank and I were staring at? The image formed from all those ones and zeros?

It was the Emerald of Astara!

ENDGAME 13

FRANK

WE *HAVE* TO CALL THE POLICE," I said for the hundredth time as we were driving through the twilit streets of Bayport on our way to the museum. We'd finalized our plans with Chet and Amber earlier. "This jewel is worth millions. It's too big to keep to ourselves."

"No," insisted Joe. "The Phantom has been leading up to this the whole time. And if he was willing to harm us when he was after swords and Civil War artifacts, just think about what he'd do to get his hands on this. He might have someone in place ready to hurt anyone we know if we go to the police. We can't risk people's lives. *We* have to finish this. That's what you said yesterday, remember?"

I sighed in frustration. In a way, I agreed with Joe. But I couldn't shake the feeling that we were pawns in a game we still didn't understand.

"I mean, why even *send* us the riddle? Why not just steal the jewel?" I asked.

"That's easy. He wants to prove he's better than us."

We parked a few blocks away from the museum. Still close enough to keep it in view, but far enough away so that it wouldn't look suspicious. It was only five o'clock, but we didn't want to be left in the lurch like last night. If the Phantom showed up early, we'd be ready.

We got out of the car and crossed the street. Since the museum was closed on Sundays, the place was deserted. We entered the empty parking lot and approached the glass doors, peering inside. Everything looked the same as it had on our school trip. I checked the walls close to the ceilings, spotting the telltale blinking red light of a motion sensor. I could also see the alarm-system keypad just inside the door. The Phantom would have to disable all that if he wanted the jewel.

We checked around the back. There was a delivery entrance there, the doors secured with a key-card reader. Huge steel trash cans and empty crates lined the walls of the lot.

"This is where he'll try to get in," Joe said.

I nodded. "We could use some of these crates to hide out in."

Joe peered into one and made a face. "I suppose. What's wrong with watching from the comfort of the car?"

"We're closer here."

Just then there was a noise behind us. We whirled around, but it was only Amber and Chet.

"We saw you guys come in," said Chet

Amber looked around. "You thinking of hiding out in these crates?"

I nodded. "But Joe wants to watch from the car."

"Shouldn't we do both?" asked Chet. "What if he tries to get in another way?"

"Good point," I said.

We decided that Chet and I would wait in the crates, while Joe and Amber would watch from each of the two cars.

Joe and Amber left to take their positions, and Chet and I shifted two of the crates so that we could see the entire back of the museum as well as the driveway that led to the front. The crates had slats wide enough for us to see out of without being spotted.

"Right," I said. "Now we wait."

If I ever write a memoir about being a detective, I'm going to be sure to mention the waiting. Sometimes I think 50 percent of the detective business is spent waiting: waiting for people to show up, waiting for clues to make sense, waiting outside buildings for people to leave. It never ends.

The hours passed and darkness fell. Streetlights flickered to life. Crickets chirped in the warmth. And we watched.

Seven o'clock rolled by. Then eight. Then nine.

The crate I was sitting in was huge, easily big enough for me to stretch out my legs, but I was still getting cramps. I was just about to risk a quick jog around the back lot when I heard something that made me freeze.

I couldn't see anything. But I had definitely heard a scuffling sound. Like a shoe on concrete.

I waited, holding my breath.

And finally saw him. He was standing in the shadows against the wall, merging seamlessly with the darkness. I carefully lifted my camera and pushed record. Using night-vision mode, I could clearly see a black-clad figure that must have been the Phantom. Chet had brought his own camera, as had Amber. Hopefully we'd get the whole night on record.

The Phantom, wearing a ski mask, stood there for about five minutes, then moved to the back entrance and crouched down. He attached a black box with wires trailing from it to the key-card reader. He fiddled with something out of sight, and a couple of minutes later stood up and opened the door.

No alarm.

I took out my phone and texted the others. HE'S INSIDE.

I climbed out of the box and hurried over to Chet. He was already getting out, having seen the Phantom as well. We moved across the lot pressed up against the wall, just in case the Phantom saw us.

Joe and Amber arrived a minute later, and all of us

moved to the door. I checked the keypad on the wall. The Phantom's gizmo was still attached to it.

We entered the museum. A few of the display cases were lit with soft glows, but that didn't really help us see; it just made everything look creepy. We moved along the corridors, passing the Ice Age exhibit, then through the Life in Victorian Times exhibit, and past the Wild West room, until we finally approached the room where the Emerald of Astara was kept.

I held my hand out to the others, signaling for them to wait while I slowly peered around the side of the door. I could see the jewel in the center of the room, lit from above by a spotlight. I breathed a sigh of relief. It was still there.

But where was the Phantom? I checked the shadows, even went up to the roof.

But he didn't seem to be here.

"What about the security room?" whispered Joe after I had reported back. "Maybe he's trying to disable the alarms for the jewel. Remember when the guide said they were separate?"

I nodded. "Anyone know where the security system is?"

"Maybe down that corridor?" Amber suggested. "The one that led to the restoration room?"

We retraced our steps, heading to the front of the building. But as we were about to pass the Ancient Egypt room, we froze.

There was banging coming from within.

Inside I could see glass cases filled with hieroglyph-covered sandstone. Sarcophagi lined the walls.

It was here that we saw the Phantom. He was tugging one of the sarcophagi open, checking inside before moving on to the next.

"What's he doing?" Chet whispered.

I shrugged and held up the camera as we all entered the room. We stood before the door so he couldn't escape.

"Turn around," I said.

The Phantom whirled around to reveal—

Jack Kruger.

He had his ski mask rolled up onto his head. His eyes were wide with shock.

"What are you doing here?" he said in amazement.

"We could ask the same thing," growled Joe. "But we *know* what you're doing."

"Then help me!" he hissed.

I lowered the camera, keeping Kruger in frame. "What?"

"Help me find him!" Kruger said.

He turned away and pulled open the next sarcophagus with a crowbar.

"Hey!" exclaimed Joe. "You're damaging them!"

"I don't care. I need to find my son!" Kruger cried.

His son? I glanced at Joe, but he looked as confused as I felt.

"You've lost us," I said. "What about your son?"

He whirled around. "You said you knew!"

"We knew you were going to break in here to steal the Emerald of Astara!"

"I have no idea what you're talking about! I got a text message. Someone calling me by my old name. It said Lance was sealed inside one of these sarcophagi. That I only had an hour to save him! Look!"

He fumbled for his phone and showed us the screen. Sure enough, there was a picture of the guy we'd seen at the window of Kruger's house shoved into a sarcophagus. His eyes were closed. I shook my head in confusion. This made no sense at all.

Kruger glared at me, his face twisted in anger. "Other than Trethaway, you're the only two who knew who I was. *You* did this. Why?" He took a threatening step forward.

"Hey, we have no idea what you're talking about," said Joe. "You're the one who threatened our family. You've been sending us riddles, trying to steal treasures. Just give it up. We've caught you!"

Kruger stared at us. Then he turned to the next sarcophagus and fiddled with the lid. It was empty, just like the others.

"Lance!" he shouted. He put his ear to the next one. "Lance!"

I looked around nervously. He was shouting, his voice filled with panic. It looked as if he was telling the truth.

I put away the camera and went to one of the last three sarcophagi. "Help me," I said to Chet.

Chet was about to argue, but he saw the look on my face and decided against it. He helped me pry open the lid while Joe and Kruger did the same with the last two.

All were empty.

"Where is he?" hissed Kruger. He turned to us. "What did you do?"

I was about to answer when an earsplitting howl echoed through the museum. The alarm!

We looked at one another in horror. I didn't even want to think about what would happen if we were caught in here. "All of us need to get out!" I shouted. "Now!"

Kruger looked around in frustration.

"Your son isn't here!" I cried. "This is the only Egyptian exhibit in the museum."

Kruger kicked one of the sarcophagi, and we sprinted from the room. The front door was closest. Kruger broke the lock with his crowbar and shoved the door open. We ran out onto the museum steps—

And what felt like one hundred spotlights erupted to life, shining directly into our faces, blinding us to anything that lay beyond.

"This is the Bayport Police Department," the familiar voice of Chief Olaf echoed. "You're all under arrest. Put your hands up and get down on your knees."

THE TRUTH 14

JOE

I DROPPED TO MY KNEES AS A FIGURE WALKED out in front of the lights, blocking some of the glare. As he approached, I saw it was Chief Olaf. He looked angrier than I'd ever seen him.

He stared down at us as if trying to understand what he was seeing. "Explain this to me. We get a tip that someone is stealing a prized French Renaissance painting, and we turn up here to find you four."

French Renaissance painting? The Renaissance exhibit was at the other end of the museum. Then the rest of his words registered. *Four* of us? I looked around and realized that Amber had managed to escape. That was something, at least.

"It's not what it looks like," said Frank.

Chief Olaf turned to him. "Really? Then the story you tell me at the station is going to have to be pretty amazing, Frank." He shook his head. "What are your parents going to say?"

I gulped. He was right. This looked *incredibly* bad for us. No matter how we tried to explain it, we had been caught red-handed breaking into the museum.

The alarm was still going off. Chief Olaf frowned and turned to his crew. "Can someone stop that alarm and kill the lights?"

After the searchlights had winked out, I blinked furiously and looked around, wishing suddenly that the harsh glare was still hiding everything from sight.

Olaf signaled for officers to come forward. "Cuff them," he ordered.

As soon as he said these words, Frank shot to his feet and grabbed hold of Chief Olaf's arm.

"Chief, please don't arrest us. There's a perfectly good explanation for this, I promise."

Olaf tried to pull away, but Frank held on tight. In fact, he moved in closer, grabbing a surprised Chief Olaf by the shoulders.

What was Frank doing? This wasn't like him.

"We'll do anything," he pleaded. "Just don't put us in jail!"

Chief Olaf managed to pry Frank's hands off his uniform. "Come on, Frank. You know how this has to go."

Frank hung his head. Olaf cuffed his hands in front of

him and led Frank to a police van parked just beyond the squad cars. I was next. I climbed into the back of the van and sat next to Frank. Then came Chet and Kruger.

The doors slammed shut, and a small light flickered to life above us.

"Well," I said. "That could have gone better."

"I still don't get it," Frank said to Kruger, all worry and fear suddenly gone from his face. "How were you going to get the jewel? How did you disable the alarms?"

"I told you, I have no idea what you're talking about."

"Then you're saying you *really* haven't been sending us riddles over the past few days?" Frank pressed.

"No! How many times can I tell you the same thing?"

"You didn't try to steal ancient samurai swords?" I asked.

"The Civil War artifacts?" added Chet.

"No!"

We fell into a confused silence. Kruger seemed like he was telling the truth. And that photograph was the real thing. But how? Was it Trethaway after all? But then where was he?

"I'll tell you one thing," said Kruger. "You asked about disabling the alarms? If I was going to steal the jewel, I wouldn't need to."

"Why?" I asked.

"Because they're already going off. If I was going to steal anything, I'd have set a few people up as a distraction, sent the police off to a different section of the museum, and I'd be in there right now, calmly plucking the jewel while every-one thinks the crime has been stopped."

My eyes went wide with amazement. I looked at Frank and saw him working furiously at his cuffs.

"What are you doing?"

Frank smiled and held up his cuffs, now unlocked. Then he held up the keys that Olaf always kept hooked to his belt. "All that stuff with Chief Olaf just now? 'Please don't arrest us. Don't put us in jail'? I grabbed his keys at the same time."

Frank unlocked my cuffs, and I passed the keys to Chet. Frank opened the back door of the van and peered out.

"Where are you going?" said Chet. "You're going to get into *more* trouble."

Frank didn't answer, slipping out of the van instead. I followed him. The police were chatting in a cluster around the front of the museum.

We ran down the street, staying in the shadows, then crossed and doubled back, slipping down the side driveway that led to the back of the building. I thought I heard Chet huffing and puffing behind us, but I couldn't see in the darkness.

Frank and I rounded the corner. If what Kruger had said was true, then the culprit—and it looked like it was Trethaway at this point—would use the back entrance to escape.

We made our way past the crates to the still-open door. As we arrived, a figure was hurrying toward us. Ready to tackle, I pulled up short when I saw it was Amber.

She stopped suddenly when she saw us, her eyes wide.

Then she ran forward and hugged me. "Thank goodness you're safe!"

She released me, then ran past us, heading for the driveway that led to the front of the museum.

"Wait!" I called. "You can't go out there. The police!"

"Did you see anyone else inside?" asked Frank.

"No," she said. "Just me. When the alarm went off, I hid. By the time I caught up to you guys, you'd already gone outside. The police were there, and I—"

"It's fine," I cut her off. "But you need to find another way out."

"Hey, Amber," said a voice from behind. "Wait up! This thing's heavy."

A second figure ran out of the museum, stumbling to a halt when he saw us.

It was Lance, Kruger's son. And he was holding the Emerald of Astara!

The four of us froze. I looked at Lance, then at Frank, then at Amber, realization slowly dawning.

"You . . . ," I whispered.

It had never been Kruger *or* Trethaway. The Phantom was Amber. Well, Amber and Kruger's own son!

"You guys are pretty good," said Lance. "I didn't think you'd get any of the riddles, but Amber said you would. Hey, can you settle something for us? She swore she didn't help you crack them. Is that right?"

"It . . . that's right," I said distantly. I couldn't believe this. We had been played right from the beginning!

"But why?" demanded Frank. "Why us? Why go to all this trouble?"

"And how do you two even know each other?" I asked.

Amber sighed and exchanged glances with Lance. "I guess after all this, you guys deserve to hear the real story." She flashed an evil grin. "After all, it won't really matter when you're behind bars for stealing the emerald."

Frank and I stood, stone-faced. We've been in this business long enough to know when someone's just trying to intimidate us.

"We're brother and sister," Amber continued. "Except Kruger doesn't know about me. Mom got pregnant with me just before he was caught. She never told him. She wanted a clean break. A new life. Lance was two at the time. They were divorced a year later. She tried to keep the truth hidden from me—from us—but I found out."

"How?" I asked.

"She kept mementos. Letters. Newspaper clippings. I guess deep down she still cared about him. Or she wanted to remember what he was like. I don't know. When I found out who our dad really was, I told Lance."

"I got in touch with Dad when he got out of prison," continued Lance. "Of course, Mom didn't know. I told him I wanted to connect with him. That I just wanted to hear stories. To find out how he did it all. I could tell he didn't want to tell me. But I told him the only time I felt close to him was when he was explaining the past." Lance shook his head. "He's such a loser."

He frowned and took a step forward. "And why go through all this trouble?" He shook his head, his eyes angry. "To make you pay. Your dad tore our family apart. Do you know what it did to my mother? It *ruined* her! We wanted to make *your* family feel the same kind of pain. The two of you and Dad are going to take the fall for this." He held up the jewel. "Of course, this won't ever be found. And the police will be pretty irritated that you won't tell them where you stashed it. But, you know, that's life."

"You set your own father up?" I asked in disbelief.

"So? What's he ever done for me?" Lance snarled. "For us?"

"He learned his lesson," said Frank. "He wanted to start fresh."

"Tough." Lance tried to push past me, but I stood my ground. He was big, though—a lot bigger than me.

"Get out of my way!"

"No." I stood firm.

"Joe," said Amber quietly. "Do as he says."

"No. You're both coming with us to Chief Olaf. We're going to tell him the truth."

Lance burst out laughing. "Oh, is that what we're going to do? And you think he'll believe you?"

"Maybe not," said a voice behind us.

I turned to see Chet appear around the corner. He was sweating, his face red. He bent down to pick something up.

"But he'll believe this," he continued, holding up his camera.

"Everyone up against the wall," shouted Chief Olaf, appearing around the corner. He was followed by the other officers. Lance tried to make a run for it, but he was tackled to the ground, screaming and shouting at the officer who pinned him.

In the confusion, Amber tried to slip inside the museum.

"Uh-uh, Amber," I said, grabbing her arm.

"Come on, Joe," she whispered. "Just let me go. For old times' sake? You always were my favorite."

"Yeah, somehow I don't believe that. Chief Olaf!" I called. "This girl and her brother are responsible for burning that painting. They also tried to steal the Emerald of Astara."

"Actually," said Frank, picking something up off the ground, "they didn't *try* to steal it. They did."

He handed the emerald to the chief. Olaf looked at it in amazement, then stared at Frank and me.

"You're still coming to the station. Until this is sorted out, everyone's under arrest. Heck, the way things are standing right now, maybe I should arrest myself and my officers, too."

Chet handed over the video camera. "I think this will explain everything," he said.

"It sure better."

The next three hours were spent sitting in the Bayport Police Department interview room, telling our story over and over while Chief Olaf wrote everything down in the police report. He made Frank, Chet, and me explain how exactly we'd cracked the riddles—right down to our thought processes at the time. Honestly, I think he was a little impressed we'd actually solved the puzzles.

"Not bad," he grudgingly said once it was all done. "Some solid detective work there."

"Thanks, Chief," I said, shocked. That might have been the first time Chief Olaf had actually complimented us.

"Of course, I would have solved the case more quickly if you'd just come to me like you promised you would."

"We're sorry about that," said Frank. "But the threat against our family . . . we couldn't risk it. You understand, don't you?"

The chief grunted. I wasn't sure if that was a yes or a no, but then he told one of his men to give us a lift back to the museum so we could pick up our cars, so it seemed it was a yes after all.

"I'm glad that's over," said Chet as we watched the police car drive away. "I haven't had a decent night's sleep in three days."

"And you won't sleep tonight either. Remember, we have school tomorrow."

Chet groaned. "Thanks for reminding me. I'll see you around."

He waved and headed back to his car. I turned and stared up at the museum.

"You okay?" asked Frank.

"Yeah, I guess. I just feel like an idiot, that's all."

"You and me both."

"What do you think will happen to Lance and Amber?"

Frank sighed. "They've had a tough life, by the sounds of it. I'm sure that will be taken into consideration. Amber is too young for real prison, though. Juvenile detention for her."

"Guess they really did follow in their father's footsteps. Poor guy. All he wanted was to start again. Can you imagine how he must be feeling right now?" I shook my head.

"He made his choices," said Frank. "I feel bad for him, sure, but no one forced him into crime."

"I suppose. Hey, Dad's coming back tomorrow. I wonder if we can convince him to take us out for deep-dish pizza. We can bribe him with the story of our case."

Frank laughed. "Maybe he can use it in one of his books."

"How cool would that be? *The Hardy Boys: Chip Off the Old Block.*"

"Not exactly a catchy title, is it?" Frank unlocked the car door. "You coming?"

"Sure." I climbed into the car. "At least one good thing came out of tonight."

"What's that?" Frank asked, starting the engine.

"It wasn't Trethaway *or* Kruger. So neither of us lost the bet."

Frank laughed. "Always looking on the bright side," he said, and we headed home.